Printed in the United States of America

Rebellious Valkyrie Press, 2016

ISBN 978-1-943773-21-3 (eBook, 2nd edition)

ISBN 978-1-943773-22-0 (paperback, 2nd US edition)

ISBN 978-1-943773-44-2 (paperback, 2nd INTL edition)

Cover Design by Untold Designs Romance and Fantasy Covers

https://www.facebook.com/untolddesignscovers/

Copyediting by R.A. Weston

http://www.rawestoneditorial.com

We want to hear from you!
Write us at guinevere.libertad@gltomaswrites.com to discuss
your fave stories by us! Comments, Suggestions, even requests
what you'd like to see in our next publications!

Also, if you loved this book, please consider leaving a review. It
really makes an authors day to read them and they're so, so
helpful in determining if this is the sort of read for the next
reader who may stumble across it. You can do so by clicking
here. And remember no review is too short!

SUMMARY:

If Teddy's dark secret is discovered, even her wealth and good looks won't save her.

When Asher Rose met Teddy King, he knew it'd be trouble, but it was just the kind of trouble he didn't mind falling in. What he hadn't planned on was falling hard for the girl no one could tame.

Strap yourself in for a sexy ride fill of intensity and disaster that spirals all the way down.

*F*THS ends on a cliffhanger ending and concludes with Friends That Still...*

CHAPTER ONE

Asher

"I'm about to wipe the floor with your ass."

More balls on the pool table meant more options for a perfectly planned-out strategy. I was going to make Reggie regret all those cheap beginner shots.

I studied where the cue ball might go with each simple move, but the harder one to pocket left me in a better position. Keeping my attention open gave me a better chance at nailing the next shot, something I was counting on.

"Seriously…hurry the fuck up, Asher."

I snickered, hunched over to catch his reaction. Of course Reggie was anxious. He was a few moves from losing.

"You're lucky we're not playing for money. By now you'd be broke."

Reggie had scratched his last move, which allowed me to move the ball freely to my advantage. It was about to get ugly quick.

"Game, punk," I taunted.

Reggie and I worked together. Not saying we were best

friends or anything, but we were boys. Mostly we smoked together, but when one of us was trying to get into something, no doubt I was the first he'd ask or vice versa. In Miami, there was always something to get into. Unfortunately, tonight wasn't one of those nights.

"Watch that next game. I'm coming for you." Reggie said. I doubled over, unable to control the laughter. It wasn't *that* funny, but it messed with his game, and I wasn't loyal. It was an average off-day, looking for stuff to do, with no money to do it.

Besides shooting hoops, playing pool, or club hopping, there wasn't much else to do when you were broke until payday. Unless you counted getting high and video games.

"I'm tired of whooping your ass. I need a minute to reflect," I said. I was so bored out of my mind that everything in the room seemed to grab my attention but the table.

During the week, not that many people showed up around here, unlike the weekend, when you could have your pick of any type of person you wanted. Not that I was looking to hook up, but I never passed up an opportunity. Parties were easiest, clubs next, but you could never sleep on raves. Here? The options were fucking slim.

"I have to go to the bathroom," Reggie said as he laid his stick down on the table.

A smirk cracked at the side of my lip ring. "All right, honey, don't fall in."

Reggie laughed it off, followed by "Fuck you, I'll be back" as he left to hit the bathroom. It was almost nine-thirty, and this place was damn near empty with exceptions of a few regulars and couples who were already out on dates. As soon as Reggie got back, I planned on suggesting somewhere more hype, or at least a place where the music was better. But the moment I turned around, I saw more than enough reason to stay put for a little while longer. From a distance, she was cute, but most girls looked cute far away. It was obvious from the way she flung her hands around that the guy sitting next to her brought her to a point of frustration. Even I could tell she wasn't interested, but judging by his grin, the guy wasn't catching the hint. Reggie got back, and an instant rush of conviction surged through me, all-in for that next game. I didn't care if it was only for a second, I wanted to get a glimpse of her up close.

"Down for another game? Or are you good?"

Reggie shook his head, smiling, so my wins had clearly gotten to him. He gathered the balls from the pockets, racking them in the middle of the table. Stealing a glance back in her direction, I tried to play cool as I noticed her approaching. For a second, I thought she was coming up to me, but as soon as she was close enough, she grabbed Reggie's arm.

"You should act like you're with me. Dude at the bar can't catch a clue." The two knew each other—why didn't that surprise me? My brows shot up when he kissed her, so seeing as how she didn't hit him, she could've been his girl.

"Damn, are you going to introduce me?" I asked as they both laughed. Reggie put his around her, devouring her short frame.

"Ash, this is Teddy. Teddy, Ash." Teddy reached for my hand to shake. The view from here answered all my questions. There was no doubt about it—girl was bad…as…fuck. Not model-thin, but carried her weight well. Miami made good on its hot weather, having all the girls in crop tops most of the year. Her skin tone was a deep brown, with the most gorgeous dark eyes I'd seen all week, and the way she switched from English to Spanish hinted at Caribbean heritage. She was Black. She could've been Cuban or Dominican or even Haitian if she just knew Spanish just from around the way.

"Hey, what's up? Sorry to break up your little date, but the dude at the bar was looking for someone stupid. I had to get out of there."

From the way she carried herself, she was used to the attention. No girl looked that good and didn't know it. "So…is this your girl?" A question I assumed had an easy answer. Teddy brought her hand to her mouth, hiding a laugh. Reggie on the other hand? If a person can burn a hole through flesh from a stare alone, Reg was attempting to now.

"No, we're just friends," Teddy said.

I balanced the pool stick behind my neck, between my shoulders. "Sorry for asking."

Teddy pulled up a chair not far from the table and sat across from us, laying her jacket on the back of it.

"So what you two getting into? I wanted a shot, and it is well-needed after that *quimbao* at the bar. You guys down?"

"No, Teddy, not everyone has money to blow," Reggie said.

"What if I bought the first round?" she asked with a wicked smile. Reggie wasn't about to speak for me. I was ready to get wasted.

"I don't turn down opportunities to get fucked up. Count me in."

Reggie shrugged, peer pressure altering his decision. "I mean, I guess. If you're buying."

Teddy jumped out her chair, with a smile that never faltered, surely counting on one of us caving in. "I'll be right back."

When Teddy left for the bar, it was hard not to notice what she was working with. "Damn. What is she eating to be shaped like that?" I dragged under a breath.

Reggie was suddenly in a sour mood. "Ash, shut up."

"My bad. She's gorgeous. Assumed that was all you."

Reggie scratched the back of his head and spoke lower under the music of the jukebox. "I am, but it isn't like... I'll explain later," Reggie grunted before dropping it all together. What did Reggie have to hide? Teddy seemed nice. There'd have to be a whole lot wrong with her to be on some bullshit like that.

* * *

Teddy

It didn't take long to catch the attention of the bartender. The guy gave top priority to the ones who spoke Español, so I didn't waste time employing the help of my parent's mother tongue. It was a good thing I saw Reggie when I did. The loser from earlier was long gone, leaving me free to make my rounds without the nuisance of getting hit on.

The plan wasn't to go out tonight. I didn't have a ton of girl-friends I could call up to accompany me in search for a spot without waiting in a line out the door just for a stab at a decently mixed drink. I'd been this close to hitting up a package store on my way home only to realize I didn't want to drink alone. A billiards bar may not have been the most ideal place to go, but it was the closest dive to my house that served alcohol without a dress code or a twenty-dollar door fee, so imagine my surprise running into a familiar face.

I wanted to drown in 151. Keeping things down were still a number one problem for me, but drinking sometimes helped me sleep. I was a social drinker after all, it was pure luck running into Reggie. I hadn't seen him in weeks and was ashamed to admit I was a little sweet on him. *Thank god it was just a little.*

A few hookups over the few months we'd known each other didn't make us more than friends with benefits, and with the pressure off, I wasn't trying to be anything more. Reggie was gorgeous, but I was worried about myself too much to be worried about a guy. Besides, we'd had a talk about being exclusive a while back, and neither one of us was ready to fold.

Reggie was that corny kind of cool, where both Kendrick Lamar and Hootie & the Blowfish made an appearance on his playlists. When I'd first met him, I'd thought he was Afro-Cubano like me because he was trying to hit on me in Spanish. Which didn't help, because I preferred African American guys to Afro-Latinos anyway. Don't ask me why, but I was like that. People were always attracted to those different than them, and I was no exception. With Reggie, we had fun. There were no plans of changing that anytime soon.

Once I considered the options, two shots apiece were way better than one. Drinking alone was not my idea of a good time, so taking shots with a group sounded like the ideal way to waste the next hour. I asked for salt and lime wedges, since taking shots was no fun without the essentials. It wasn't until my way back when I really got a good look at the white boy that Reggie was with.

Ash…ton? Ash…er?

From first glance, I didn't know what to make of him. His left arm was covered in a sleeve of tattoos, a clear observation from his grey baseball jersey. His other arm was halfway there, but it wasn't as decorated as the other, but I took it that he just wasn't done yet. The guy had a load of piercings, including an eye-grabbing one on his lower left lip. Not that I was looking, but if I were? I'd say it brought a lot of attention to his mouth.

"Damn, girl, you're trying to get hammered."

I chuckled before laying the shot tray on the table. Reggie and his friend were quick to devour the first shot, so I followed suit.

"I hope you aren't driving, Teddy," Reggie felt the need to press before his friend took the next shot to the head. I already liked him.

"I can handle my liquor, thank you," I sneered. Reggie was one to talk. He was a lightweight, often getting messed up over two drinks. His friend, on the other hand, seemed like the perfect chill partner, ready for anything.

"Damn, that 151 man. Shit burns the whole way down." Reggie's friend stuck out his tongue, and I noticed his tongue ring. Hmm…

I handed Reggie his last shot, but he turned it away. "I'm not trying to get drunk, Teddy. I'm driving," Reggie said, as his friend reached for it. I laughed and pulled it away.

"Hey, I'll take it if he doesn't want it."

My lips curled in a devious smile. "You guys are no fun. You're supposed to do body shots when you're in a group. Those are unwritten rules."

Reggie clucked, shaking his head. "Teddy, you're corny."

I pointed to the last two shots. "There's two left. You *have* to do a body shot."

Reggie stretched out on the pool table, exposing himself, with the drink on his crotch. His friend burst out laughing.

"Hell no, motherfucker."

I grabbed the shot and gestured to my chest. "If it makes it easier, you can do it on me," I flirted.

Now that I was closer, there was no way to ignore his friend was gorgeous. His eyes were lethal, a sort of gunmetal blue that gleamed with a little danger above that five o'clock shadow sprouting from his chiseled cheeks. Chestnut-colored strands spilled out of his scalp in a side-swept undercut, with just a few streaks of dark blonde to complete his unconventional style. He was working it, though. You didn't see too many skater types rocking Timbs and baseball-style jerseys.

He shook his head, laughing between me and Reggie. "I'm not trying to make shit awkward."

I sucked my teeth, screw face and all. "Oh, please, it's a body shot, not a marriage proposal."

All he managed to do was shrug. "Okay." If I wasn't mistaken, Reggie was totally the jealous type, but with us? Had no reason to be. Since we'd known each other, we'd always been each other's side flings. Maybe not the main ones, but I was surprised when he didn't flinch at the idea of his friend taking a body shot off me. That fact only made me more curious about Asher.

"So where you want me to start? Like…"

I pointed to my neck as he anchored in. I burst out laughing the minute his pierced tongue licked my throat. He smiled. Did I forget to mention I was ticklish?

"See?"

"No. no. I'm cool, go ahead." I giggled, arching my neck to give him a better view. If Reggie was jealous, he didn't show it, but my heart beat faster when Asher's tongue came in contact with my skin again.

"Not too much salt now."

"You're the boss."

I placed the lime wedge between my teeth, and the shot glass in the swell of my cleavage, so glad I was wearing a bomb-ass lift bra today. Of course Reggie just had to say something.

"Teddy, you're fucking crazy."

"Don't get mad you're a lightweight. Old one-shot-having ass." His friend took a second to shake the salt on my neck and held his hands up defensively.

"Now, before I reach in, you good? I'm not trying to get snuffed."

"Boy, shut up."

He laughed it off, leaning in to lick the salt from my neck for the third time. The warmth of his tongue sent sparks to the spot, while the steel of the barbell ring sent chills. He didn't hesitate to take the shot glass, so when he leaned in for the wedge, I held onto it, his lips curling against mine. He struggled for a second, not yet willing to pull away, but as he did, the lime wedge went with him.

Reggie hadn't even been paying attention, busy on his phone, distracted in conversation. If he had, who's to say he would've thrown a fit at the sight of me kissing his friend? Was it really a kiss? One could argue that it was just an innocent exchange during a drinking game. The moment Asher's eyebrow cocked, assessing me with a sin-filled gaze, I knew he'd been wondering the same thing. He chucked the lime wedge from his teeth.

"You're cool as fuck. Trying to figure out how the hell you know Reg." Reggie's call didn't last long, but I was crap at answering questions. I was more curious to know the deal between the two of them.

"How do you two know each other?"

"We work at the same place," Reggie said, leaning on the table. "*A job*, Teddy, something you wouldn't know anything about.".

Reggie never missed an opportunity to point out the fact I didn't have a job. I was a borderline trust-fund kid, so the truth was I'd never even held a part-time job. When my parents came to the United States, they had their eyes set on living the American dream. My mom was an electrical engineer; my papi, a cardiologist. I suppose I reaped the benefits of their success. They paid for my condo, my car, and most of my bills, anything to keep the stress off me for the time being. Sometimes I think they worried too much about me. I had health issues, but I don't know. I guess if I were a parent that went through half as much as they had, I'd worry myself to death about my child's health, too.

"Whatever. I'm bored. After this shot, I was going to head home and burn one, but if you two aren't doing anything—"

"You got weed? Why didn't you say so? Fuck sitting here!" Asher jumped in.

Reggie didn't rush to get up. In fact, he didn't look thrilled to tag along. I patted the back of my bun and slipped back into my jacket. "Well?" I asked, but was it really smart to have Reggie over? Any time we met back at my place, we'd had problems keeping our clothes on. Sometimes it was all me, sometimes all him, but if it counted for anything, his friend being present would probably prevent any hook-ups from happening.

"I can't stay long. I have to drop Ash off and the car, but we'll meet you at your place. Sound cool?"

I rolled my eyes and nodded. "Don't take too long. Otherwise I'll have to invite some other dudes over to get faded with."

I waved them both goodbye when they followed me out to the parking lot. I needed to make a pit stop, but in the next few minutes, I was amped to get this party started.

* * *

Asher

The drive wasn't long to her place, but Reggie got there before she did. We spent the whole car ride bullshitting about the Spurs vs the Heat, Reg hardly mentioning Teddy at all.

"So where'd you meet homegirl?"

Reggie grunted, rolling his wrist against the steering wheel. "It's kind of a short story," Reggie said, which meant I shouldn't have asked. Reg wasn't in the mood to talk about it, but there didn't seem to be much to discuss. Looks aside, Teddy seemed like a really cool girl. Hell, I wish I would've met her first.

"Damn, she live on the nice side of Edgewater. She bunkin'?"

Reggie snorted, rubbing his face in a fit of laughter. "No, dumbass. Her parents? Refined, rich and Republican." He counted off with three fingers, with that last one resulting in a grimace from me. After much debate, he claimed they were pretty liberal, if that could even co-exist with the word. "From what she says, her parents are like doctors, engineers or some shit."

"Okay? So what's the problem again?"

Reggie clucked his teeth, facing me. "Teddy…is a handful. More trouble than it's worth. Don't get me wrong, she's cool to be around…sometimes. But she's the kind of girl who gets you fucked up over her and then she pulls the rug from under you. Weeks at a time she don't call you. Always ready to argue. I don't fuck with her like that. She doesn't take anything seriously."

Something wasn't adding up.

"Let me get this straight? She's bad. She smokes. She likes to party. And she doesn't need money, so you don't have to buy her anything. I'll get back to you on that Republican thing, but outside of that, what's the fucking problem again?"

Reggie collapsed his weight to the back of his seat, rubbing the temples on his forehead. "You don't know Teddy like I do. We have fun together, but she's just not girlfriend material."

"Dude, this is why you're single. Too fucking picky."

"I know you're not talking."

"I'm not picky. You always want life-sized Barbies, with perfect bodies, perfect attitudes, coming off an assembly line. I just like someone who's available. Doesn't hurt when she looks like that."

"I know where this is going, and I'm not having this conversation again. What's wrong with a girl who's in shape? I can have a pre-requisites of who I stick my dick into, you know. Unlike you."

I scratched my cheek, resting my arm on the open window. "Well, I'm not banging chicks like that no more. I get burned too much not being careful of who I end up with. If I'm not suited up for battle, the cavalry isn't going to war. And what you got against big girls? I know some girls that look good that just happen to *not* be a size six. Keep your options open, man. Open your horizons."

Teddy's car pulled up in the driveway just in time to cut the conversation short. Reggie laughed it off, but seriously, he was way too picky. Now was the time to date a swarm of different kinds of people. I was twenty-two—I liked to get reckless. Far from a player, but a lot happened when you lived by one simple mantra: You only live once.

Reggie only wanted *certain* girls. In other words, the girls that were boring as hell. I liked people I had to worry about. You couldn't control heartbreak, so what was the point in trying? Besides, you know what they say. Love is never fun if the ride is dull and tame.

* * *

Teddy

By the time I got to my place, I was ready to be comfortable. I'd braided my long kinky hair into a milkmaid style and slipped on some flannel pajama pants and matching slippers.

Meaningless banter and endless teasing traveled through my living room walls from all the way here in the hallway. With my bedroom door open just a crack, it was enough to peek in on Reggie and his friend Asher trading off on trivial topics. Reggie was more my type *physically*, but I couldn't help but find Asher interesting and that in itself made me curious. Where Reggie stood taller than me at five-foot-eight, Asher towered over him at six-foot-two. I liked that. Height didn't make anyone better-looking, but in Asher's case, it was definitely one of his strong points. I'd probably get myself in trouble for acting on it, but thinking dirty thoughts about the guy wasn't wrong, was it?

* * *

Asher

If Teddy lived here by herself, her parents were doing well. I shared an apartment with three roommates, and it looked like shit in comparison.

The walls were painted a light blue, while the sleek furniture and pop art paintings had this place resembling an apartment store showroom. There were about seven decked-out bookcases overflowing, along with the Cuban flag hidden in subtle places around her house. A whimsical hand-lettered print that read *Una Afro-Cubana vive aqui* hung up along her wall, confirmed my suspicion of her background.

Teddy stepped into the living room looking hotter now than she had a few minutes ago. Her hair was braided up and away from her face, but if you asked me to name the style, I couldn't. She sat down in the chair across from the loveseat as I browsed her mini-library. I'd never seen this many books in my life that belonged to one person. And judging by the covers, all fiction.

"I'm guessing you like to read?"

"Yeah, but she's into all that creepy shit. Horror, science fiction, freaking *Final Fantasy* or some shit," Reggie answered for her. "You won't find a normal book on any of those shelves, and what's worse is that they're all by black people. I don't even know any black folk into all that."

Teddy rolled her eyes and explained to me that she was a huge Black speculative fiction fan and it's what her shelves reflected. Names like Tananarive Due and Octavia Butler sprang out at me, but I had no idea who any of them were. Still, it was cool that she liked to read. The only thing I read nowadays were emails and updates. I may give one of these ones a try one day.

She moved to the floor to fill up the paper, rolled a joint, and used a lighter to take the first hit. Her lips enveloped the joint, and she blew out residue smoke. I sat next to her and she handed it to me to take the next hit.

"Fair warning—I got vacuum lungs. I doubt there'll be shit left when I get to it."

"I wish you would've mentioned that when we were at the pool hall," she joked, leaning onto her palm, her back to the couch. She must've had Indica because she was super chill. I preferred the high from Sativa, but both took me to different places. This definitely had me feeling couch-locked. All I'd have the energy to do was play video games all night.

First round of *puff, puff, pass* ended with Reggie. Reg wasn't like me—he wouldn't do anything harder than weed. But when the opportunity presented itself, it was his public duty to always be down to smoke.

"Damn, Teddy, you be havin' that good kush," Reggie said, dazing off. Teddy giggled her ass off, kicking her feet onto the couch. I'd leave this out to Reggie, but everything she did, was doing, and probably would do if no one stopped her, was sexy as hell. She was a little out of my league, but it didn't stop the daydreaming.

Reggie wasn't exactly swimming in girls, so here she was, this beautiful girl, all over him, and dude didn't even appreciate it. She crawled over me to Reggie's lap.

"Damn, do you guys need a room?"

Teddy sucked her teeth, making a shooing gesture with her hands. "It's not like you care," she said, reaching in to meet Reggie's lips. Reggie pulled her off of him.

"Teddy, stop. If you want do something, can we go to your room? You know I'm not for all that public shit."

I just doubled over in a guffaw of laughter. Teddy rolled her eyes.

"You know what? Just for that, we don't have to do anything." She got up and walked to her room, slamming the door. Reggie gave me a side-eye as if saying, *See what I mean?* But I didn't care. I was already lifted and it wasn't my problem. No need to fuck up my high.

"Let's get the hell out of here before it gets too late." I grabbed my hoodie as we saw our way out.

CHAPTER TWO

Asher

It was four minutes before five when my feet made it to that time clock. The first of the month was always busy working at a grocery store, and running the front end didn't make it any easier. When customers wanted to complain about prices, cashiers, or something completely out of my control, like lines, guess who they came to? Me.

"Asher, you're leaving?" my coworker Sean asked as he approached. I hated that. When people asked questions with such obvious answers. I'm standing *by* the time clock, I'm in my street clothes, and I look just about ready to start jumping hurdles over these shopping carts before my manager Steve can con me into staying another hour. What does he think I'm standing here for? Concert tickets?

"Yeah, man, eight-thirty to five. I'm done with this place," I said, trying to drag out these last few minutes.

"Yeah I know what you mean. Soon as I leave here, I'm off to my third job."

"Got more jobs than a Jamaican," I bantered. We shared a

laugh and next thing I knew it was time to go. Happy to be out this place, even if it was just for the day.

"Heyyyyy, Asher," Vicky said, blocking me just moments before I reached the store's entrance.

"Heyyyy, Vicky," I said in a mimicking tone. Vicky was a cashier here, and the perfect example that a girl with a few extra pounds could be equally sexy. She was sort of a "blonde" and super high-strung. Sometimes it was hard keeping her attention for more than a few minutes.

"Coming to my party tonight?" she asked pulling her cell phone out of her oversized bag.

Vicki lived in a one of the few houses left standing in Edgewater, Miami, so her parties were always super epic and hype. I wasn't doing shit tonight. Looked like I'd found the answer to my boredom blues.

* * *

The moment I walked through the door of my apartment, my phone rang, interrupting a do-or-die challenge round of *Trivia Crack*. Reggie's name lit up my screen. This had better be good.

"Yo," I dragged out.

"You left work so fast. I needed you to do something for me."

I passed two of my roommates on the way to my room, prepared to tell Reggie a big fat no on a favor. I only had a few hours to sleep before I got cleaned up for Vicky's party tonight. There wasn't anything he could say that could get me out of this bed right now.

"I need you to buy me a half. You know Lala don't fuck with me like that, but she's the only one that got that kush I like. I'll hit you off with a quarter if you do this for me."

Damn, just when I was about to get comfortable. I had zero willpower when it came to turning down anything free. "Beep the horn when you're outside."

Reggie pulled up in his old grandmother's beater. The dude flapped his mouth constantly about needing to get his own car, but with his part-time hours and his part-time checks, chances were that wasn't happening anytime soon. Even at full-time I wasn't making it rain, but I was doing better than most folks I knew. Never missed a utility or rent payment and had plenty of cash to throw around on my vices, so I couldn't complain. What I didn't need was a car. My street legal took me pretty much everywhere I needed to go, and I didn't go through fifty bucks of gas money like I would've with a car. Maybe in the future when I had a solid reason to own one, but for now it was just me and my baby.

"You know you have to drive," Reggie said.

I snapped my fingers, recalling that tidbit, feeling off that I always had to be reminded. That's how it always went when we went for a run. Reggie crawled into the passenger side while I hopped into the driver's spot. I adjusted the seat to my desired level of comfort since Reggie was a six inches shorter, and it was like driving in a clown car.

"Fix my seat when you get out. I almost got into an accident last time I had you riding in this car."

I turned the radio on to some techno station and adjusted the rearview mirror, backing out of my apartment's driveway. "So you got that or…" I said, holding out my hand. He slapped a few twenties in my palms, and I looked down to count it only to find it was fifteen bucks short of Lala's regular price for a half.

"You know this is only a buck-twenty, right?"

"And?"

I laughed and stuffed it in my pocket once I reached the red light. "No wonder she don't fuck with you. For one, you tried to accuse her of selling you some whack shit, and two, you're always looking for discounts. Shit, I don't even like fucking with you."

"You know that girl is sweet on you. She don't fuck with nothing but white-looking boys. Play that card."

I laughed. Reggie was always talking some dumb shit, but it wasn't a lie. She *did* have a thing for me. It was worth a shot trying. The worst she could say was no.

I dropped Reggie off around the corner because if she even caught a glimpse of him, she'd give me a hard time buying. The routine was simple. He picked me up, I dropped him off a few blocks away, and I picked him "back" up from the corner. We blazed up, then he dropped me back off. I pulled up to see her sitting on her porch.

She was dark-skinned, kind of chubby, with sisterlocks down to her ass rocking a hippie style maxi dress. She wasn't the kind of girl I was usually went for, but I still thought she was sexy. Especially when she spoke that Patois shit.

"Hey, beautiful," I said, my elbows rested on the window of the car. She smiled, strolling up with a smug look on her face. "Look at you... Umph. I'm saying, though, when are we going out?"

She laughed, pulling her cardigan over her exposed bust line. "Asher, you know I have a man."

I winked. "So? What's that have to do with me? You can keep him."

She shoved my shoulder playfully. "Asher, you are too much. Like *too* much. Good thing I like that about you."

"Oh, yeah? What else do you like about me?" Eyeing her up and down, I bit my lip.

"You're about to make me drop this Nicaraguan dude biting your lips like that. So what's good, what you need? A half, right?"

I hated that Reggie put me in this spot, but I was a good customer and I'd never tried to cheat her. I may not always be honest, but I was loyal when it came to this kind of thing. Trustworthy. Good for business. "Listen, I'm like fifteen short of what you usually have me for. Things were a little short this week. You think you could help me out and I got you next time?"

She crossed her arms over her chest, eyebrow cocked, and

judging by her change in attitude, undecided. "I know you're not trying to play me?"

"Lala, it's not even like that. I'm just short. You know I'm not trying to play you." She stood there, silently debating, until she finally spoke. "Wait right here." When she returned, she threw what looked like a strain I'd never seen before.

"That's some new stuff I got. I'll let you try it at a lower price since I don't know if you'd like it. But I know you. I have a feeling you will."

I brung it to my nose and inhaled its sweet scent. It wasn't dry like some weed was, and the crystals were a good sign. It wasn't my money to gamble with, but since this idiot had me out here practically begging for a price cut, I figured if he wanted a half, at least he'd get it.

"Cool," I said, forking over the cash.

"Let me know how you like it. "

"You don't have to worry. I will. In the meantime, stay sexy," I flirted with a wink. I drove off onto northwest 11th Avenue, eager to get back home to try out this new strain. I wasn't the picky type, but I had my favorites so I was reluctant to try something new on my own dime. Once I pulled onto my street, my phone rang and the thought dawned on me. I'd forgotten Reggie at that street corner.

I was *too* ready to go out tonight.

* * *

"You know Vicky's having a party tonight, right?" I said as I took a hit of Reggie's blunt. Vicky had a huge thing for Reggie, but since he didn't like plus-sized girls, he kept his distance. I couldn't think of one good reason Reggie would turn down a chance to get smashed with no door charge and free drinks all night, even if Vicky did have a crush on him.

"You know I not trying to be around Vicky like that. Girl's a

stalker, putting love letters in my locker and shit. I'm good, son."
Guess I was wrong.

"So what—you're just chill going to sit home all night while I go out and have all the fun? You're corny, you know that? That or you stuck on that Juicy Fruit." Juicy Fruit was my nickname for his homegirl. The girl his dumbass was playing games with. It didn't make sense that he wasn't trying to claim her but to each his own.

"I'm not even thinking about Teddy. That girl is always on some dumb shit. I told you, that's why I don't fuck with her like that."

"That or she don't fuck with *you* like that," I said with a laugh. It was a competition between me and Reggie on how many girls played us on a regular basis. Don't get me wrong, Reggie and me had no issues with getting girls. It was *keeping* them that was the biggest obstacle. Most girls had us out here looking stupid, and I know that ate Reggie up inside. Me? I was a more go-with-the-flow type. I tried not to put my whole being into one relationship because when I did, I fell hard.

"Well, if you're not coming with me, drop me off then. I have to get ready. I'm not doing shit tonight and I refuse to be in the house bored as hell like your whack ass."

* * *

Teddy

I'd been dancing for less than an hour and already my feet hurt. One might say my open toe shoes were the culprit, but no. It was due to all these drunk-ass wannabes trying hold their liquor, stepping on my toes. A couple of beers and already some of these people were done. How did I end up at these dumbass parties?

The DJ was spitting something fierce, a nice blend of pop, house, and dancehall making love to my eardrums. From the sound of things, this party *should* have been off the hook, but I kid you not, no one at this place looked older than twenty. It felt more like a high school dance.

There was a spot on the loveseat in the back of the room, away from the dancefloor. I thought I'd be relieved to sit but quickly regret it once I did. Why the hell were the couch cushions wet? *I* wasn't about to find out, but it didn't seem to bother the two couples flanked at the other ends of the couch. Drunk and horny were never the best pair at reason and logic. One more drink and I was out of this place. One more drink and I was done.

In the kitchen, there was the usual. A few dumb white boys drinking beer from a tube that led to a keg. Empty red cups all over the floor that screamed *"fuck it, this isn't my house,"* and an entire counter of liter-sized bottles of hard liquor, soda, and juice. Looked like it was going to be a rum-and-Coke kind of night.

I carried my cup back to the main room only to discover almost thirty more people making use of the dance floor that hadn't been there a minute ago. All of a sudden, the room felt more crowded, and the only area of solitude was a spot near the kitchen. Oh, well.

I needed to sit down again. If this was the only available seat in the room, guess my butt would be parked here for the remainder of my stay. I took out my phone, going through my messages, and shifted through my dry-ass IG timeline. I thought about taking a selfie in all this madness, but it felt like a lie to post a picture of what looked like me having fun when it couldn't be further from the truth. I needed to make some new friends.

"Hey, Asher! You made it," a perky voice cried a few feet away as I watched two people reach out to hug each other. Asher. Asher-From-the-Other-Night Asher. I was never good with names, but there was something about Ash that earned him a front row seat in my guarded memories.

Piercings, tattoos, and a hybrid style that wasn't quite skater or all the way urban. I wasn't even into alternative guys until I'd met Reggie, but checking for a guy like Asher made me question why I even had a type. The time had come to start broadening my taste in people.

Asher broke free from what I gathered was the hostess to the party. For a second, I thought he might have seen me sitting against the wall, but he walked right past me into the kitchen. A few minutes passed until I finally saw him again, cup in hand, finding a comfortable spot to lean on while he observed the crowd. What, was I invisible tonight?

I pulled at the bottom of his sweater, and he wore a confused look on his face until the look of recognition became clear. He flashed me a megawatt smile that shined bright, even in the dimly lit room, and I silently forgave him when his eyes lingered on my cleavage. He crouched down next to me, the scent of his woodsy cologne leaving its mark between us. Damn, was he looking this good the other day? Because he was definitely looking good enough to eat tonight.

"Funny seeing you here. I was just chilling with your boy."

I rolled my eyes, assuming the "boy" in question was Reggie. Um…no.

My situation with Reggie was complicated, but he was most certainly not "mine" nor was I claiming to be his. Three months ago I'd put the idea out there that I was interested in taking things to another level, and he'd done nothing short of laugh in my face. Since then, I wasn't interested in hearing *my, you, girl* or *man* in the same sentence when it came down to me and Reggie. He and I were friends for sure, but that was about all we'd be. At least until he started acting with some sense.

Asher took the cup from my hands and put it on the floor beside him. "Get up, we're dancing," he said, helping me up from the floor. It was a miracle. Suddenly I had the energy to dance and a reason to stay. And to think, if I'd left a minute earlier…

Asher had some serious moves. I felt a little unworthy in his presence when he took the lead, perfectly in tune with my swaying hips in a *perreo* as the familiar *tresillo ritmo* in the form of a Reggaeton track blared loud from the speakers surrounding us. What really surprised me was how quick he switched it up when the DJ pulled a one-eighty with a Ginuwine song. No lie, if it was between this guy and Channing Tatum in a dance-off, Asher would win hands down. The boy could dance.

"It's a good thing you came when you did. I was, like, a few songs away from leaving. No offense to the person throwing this thing, but this party's legit whack," I said over the music. The next song in queue was something slow, but still insanely loud. Why hadn't they called the cops yet?

"I was just sitting at home bored, looking for something to do tonight. Music, drinks, dancing. More than I would've been doing at home."

"Hey, you know I don't live far from here, right? I don't have a wide variety, but I've got tequila and an O at my house."

A smile curved at the side of his mouth, his tongue playing with the piercing that occupied the corner.

"What are we still doing here, then? Let's go."

I grabbed his arm and guided him through the crowd of people, the muggy air of Miami's weather in full effect the second we stepped outside. I looked at my reflection in a window of a car parked in the girl's driveway, disappointed that the humidity once again wreaked havoc on my style tonight. The "stretched" curls I'd convinced myself would stay stretched if I didn't dance too much, transformed into a shrunken afro. I hadn't even known it.

Asher walked past me and put the keys in the ignition of something that resembled a motorcycle. Maybe smaller.

"You drove?"

The engine roared as he started it up but lowered down to a

purr when he reached the end of the driveway. "Can't leave it, want a ride?"

It was a tempting offer, but I knew if I didn't at least braid it, my hair would be a tangled mess come sleep time and, when it was time for me to lay my head down, a girl got lazy.

"You remember how to get to my house, right?" He nodded. "Cool, just meet me there. I'll be there in five."

"You sure?"

I waved him off. "Yeah, I'll see you in a bit."

He shrugged half-heartedly. "Suit yourself." He speed off into the street, probably waking up the whole neighborhood with the blast his bike made on takeoff. That I couldn't worry about. I had to do something to this hair.

* * *

Asher

"Took you long enough," I said, standing up from her condo's staircase. She gave me the finger and stuck her tongue out in a childish way, but cute.

"No one told you to go ninety just to go a few streets over. It wasn't even that serious."

She gestured for me to follow. She'd braided her hair into two French braids that snaked down the length of her back, only bringing more attention to her ass, something I was trying to avoid. Tight jeans and self-control did not go well together.

"Look, I don't know what it was, but I know I sat in something at that party. I won't feel right if I don't hop in that shower. You don't mind waiting for me, right?" She laid her keys down on one of the kitchen counters, telling, not asking me.

"As long as you don't mind if I hit up this cereal," I said, pointing to a few boxes she had scattered across the counter.

"Yeah, sure. I'll try not to take forever. If you're interested, tequila's in the fridge."

A place stocked with food, liquor, and a friend open to smoke me out. I'd come up with a new nickname for Teddy's spot: Heaven.

* * *

Walking out in a bralette and shorts, Teddy looked surprisingly younger with her bare face, free of makeup. She looked nice.

"*Oh, hell no*. I know you didn't open my new box of Cheerios. You're so busy tearing up my food, did it occur to you that the one sitting eight inches away was already open?"

For a second there, I thought she was serious, but she wore a huge smile that made it hard to take her seriously.

"Oh my bad. I thought they were both new. I got you, though. It might not be brand-name though. Might be some, like, Honey-Flavored Oat Os. Some shit we have at the job. But trust me—essentially the same."

She lifted up on the balls of her feet to reach a bowl on one of the top shelves of her cabinet. I did us both a favor and got it down for her. She looked funny jumping up and down for a damn bowl.

"You're short," I snorted. "You can't even reach something in your own house."

She stuck her tongue out and reached to open the cabinet underneath. From there, she pulled out a grey and white stool and I couldn't hold back. I laughed my ass off.

"Honestly, I don't know anyone that owns one of those things. It's cute that you need one."

"Well, we can't all be Jolly Green Giant, okay? Not everyone is blessed with the gift of height."

Being short definitely wasn't a bad thing. I hated how girls thought it was. Some actually liked petite women. I just liked it all. Besides, what Teddy lacked in height, she was blessed pretty much everywhere else. Reggie was lucky as shit.

"Hey, does this hurt?" She reached up and touched my ear plugs. Between the plugs and piercings, I had about seven between both ears, most being in my right, the one she was touching.

"Nope."

"Think you'll go bigger?"

I took a deep breath, preparing my answer. I'd thought about it but stayed at seven-sixteenths for a while now with no concrete plans to go bigger anytime soon. Never say never, though.

"I don't know. Maybe."

"Do you have a lot of tattoos and piercings?"

My shoulders rose and lowered, taking one last bite of the bowl of cereal before washing it in the sink. "Guess it depends on what you mean by a lot."

She rolled her eyes back and forth. "I don't know... More than ten."

"I have fifteen piercings. Tatts—you kind of lose track after a while. I know it has to be more than ten, though. It could be twelve. It could be fifty. They all sort of blend once you start," I said pulling up the sleeves to my shirt. She looked from my arms to my eyes, regarding me with curiosity. Maybe even disdain. I was shit at reading people.

"Got a favorite?" she said, putting down her bowl despite only eating three spoonfuls. I opened my mouth, my barbell front and center as I stuck out my tongue. She bit her lip and laughed. Fucked me up for a second.

"So...how long have you known Reggie?" She walked into the living room and I took that as my cue to follow.

"I don't know. Maybe six months, something like that that. Since he started working at the job."

She sat down on the couch and patted the spot next to her. On the coffee table in front of us sat an ounce of what I hoped was some high quality weed. Even if it wasn't, I wasn't complaining when someone was the hook up. From what I remembered from last time, Teddy was good for it.

"You want to roll?" She handed me a pair of Backwoods, and I unrolled and dumped the tobacco on the plate. She got up and turned on some music. I didn't know who the artist was, but I knew it was bachata coming out of the speakers.

"You got some honey or something? I'm not trying to tongue down the blunt and shit." But she assured me she didn't mind as long as I wasn't sloppy about it. I think she just wanted to see my tongue again. Or maybe I was seeing things.

I put the tip to my lips, and she did the honors of lighting the other end. After two puffs, I passed it as she flipped one of her French braids to the back and took a hit. This went out for two more passes until the effects of Indica started to kick in. I laid back on the couch, letting the high takeover my bloodstream and take me to a place of euphoria.

"Nice rolling," she said with a sexy smile on her face. I didn't know what Reggie's problem was. Teddy was cool as hell. Way out of his league.

"So are you and Reggie close?"

I shrugged. "Close? Eh...that's reaching, but he is my boy though. Cool people." I took another hit and watched Teddy finish off the rest. "Why do you ask?"

She lay across the couch, her feet finding a comfy yet inconvenient spot in my lap. Her toes were perfectly pedicured, an absolute weakness of mine. I loved pretty feet. If she wasn't careful, she might find a toe or two in my mouth. My pants were already getting tighter at the thought of it. I needed to stop.

"I don't know. You just seem...different."

"Different?"

She buried her face in her hands and spread her fingers for her eyes to peek through. "Let's just say, me and you would've never crossed the same path in high school."

I shrugged. "I don't know why. You smoke, I smoke," I said,

pointing to myself. "You drink, I drink. I know some people in relationships that don't even have that much in common."

We both shared a laugh as she shifted her feet, one on my thigh. The other stayed put.

"I know it's just...I kind of pictured you listening to depressing music about self-mutilation and, like, puppy murder."

I laughed. "You got some dark-ass thoughts. But just for the record, I like fun music. Dubstep. Electronica. Post-hardcore EDM. Electro house. Some hip hop, too. I deejayed in high school so my taste is all over. And puppies? I like puppies. I'm not even going to sit up here and lie to you. Lassie's my shit." That made her laugh and in turn made me join in with her. Everything was ten times funnier under the influence and right about now was the chill point.

"What kind of music do you like? Like salsa, reggaeton, merengue? Stuff like that?"

She nodded. "Yeah, pretty much, but I like rock in Spanish, too. Oh and hip hop, but not any of this new stuff. Unless I'm faded. Like right about now I could probably listen to something whack and think it was, like, Tupac or something."

I didn't take her for a hip-hop fan—she was girlier than I originally took her for. But it wasn't fair to judge. After all, she'd judged me based off my tattoos and how I dressed. She was all wrong about me.

"For real, though, the album that changed my life was *Legal Drug Money* by the Lost Boyz. That shit went in."

"Really? Hmm... Until tonight, I thought you were just as whack as Reggie can be, but you're like...your own flavor. We should hang out again after this."

"Well, take my number. Hit me up." I tossed Teddy my phone and was impressed she caught it in one hand. "Let me find out you're fresh out the boat." She kicked me in the side and pointed my phone at herself at various angles. "What the hell are you doing?"

"Just for that comment, I'm going to hack your phone and make a bunch of obnoxious videos and post them to all your social networks."

I held up my hands, not willing to put up much of a fight. Why would it bother me having videos of her in my phone? She was hot, and all I'd get was lots of love if she did. She'd be doing me a favor.

"It's no fun if you don't fight me," she laughed, tossing me back my phone. Interestingly enough, we had the exact same model. She texted herself my number as well as a picture snapped of me when I wasn't looking. Teddy was stealth with it.

"So what do you, like, do?" I asked out of curiosity. I was still in awe of the way this girl could afford to live in an apartment this nice despite the fact that she had no job. Or at least from what Reggie told me. All he knew was she had an associate degree in English literature and education.

"What do you mean, like…?"

"Work? School?" I didn't know what answer I expected from her, but now that I was high, I had less of a filter.

"I don't know. I'm kind of still figuring myself out," she said, tossing her head to one side.

"Well, tell me your secret. I would love to live in an apartment like this figuring myself out," I joked.

"Don't laugh, but right now I live off my trust. Nothing huge. Just enough to cater to my expenses."

My eyes widened in awe. She hit me in the shoulder like she was too comfortable already, which was good. I liked that she was around me.

"What? I've just never actually met someone who could do that." Clearly I was born into the wrong family. I'm sure neither one of my folks had even cleaned a place this nice.

"Enough about that. I'm bored." Her lips curled into a pout as she reached for the TV's remote. "I've got Netflix and Amazon Prime. Want to watch something? I've got some bootleg DVDs over there. John Singleton and Spike Lee bundles. Six movies for like ten bucks."

I scratched my chin. "Just John and Spike, huh?"

She nodded. "I like their direction."

"Okay, fuck it then, put in *Clockers*. That's the only other one I haven't seen."

Teddy hopped off the couch and popped it in the DVD player. "Want to split another J real quick?"

With all her generosity, how could I say no?

* * *

"They are so fucked up for that," Teddy laughed while she stretched out for the second time tonight with her feet in my lap. She was so down-to-earth. At first, I'd thought it was a front. Prettier girls tended to act one way in public and another in private. Teddy was pretty much the same both ways. Things got weird when her feet rubbed against my crotch, though. I know she'd had a few drinks and was high as hell, but it was getting to a point of no return. I was getting hard, and there'd be no way to hide it.

I chewed on my fingernail in an attempt to think of other pressing topics. She turned to face me.

"Are you fucking hard right now?"

I let out a deep breath, resting my head in the palms of my hands. "My bad. It's just you have sexy-ass feet and you're, like, rubbing them on my dick. Once you stop, I *guarantee* it will *not* be an issue."

She bit her lip. "What if I don't want to stop?"

Palm up, I lifted my hand loosely. "I'm not going to tell you what to do in your own house, Teddy." Plus, it felt good. Why would I tell her to stop?

Feeling daring, I lifted up one of her feet and started sucking on her row of toes. Her legs twitched as she snatched her feet away from my mouth.

"Now you know how it feels," I said, laughing. She looked embarrassed, but I knew she'd liked it. The face she'd made before she'd caved spoke volumes.

She crawled up next to me, and if things weren't awkward enough, she straddled me. She leaned in to kiss me, and just as I suspected, her lips felt as soft as they looked. Lips like hers were always the best to kiss. She drew them in a line from my ears to the middle of my neck, igniting a low moan from me. She had me hypnotized, making me forget who I was kissing for a second.

Teddy. The same Teddy who was tight with my boy. Hooking up with him, too. I knew they weren't serious, but it felt like I was crossing a line here. "Wait, wait. Teddy…what are we doing?"

She ran her fingers through my hair and unleashed a small smile. It was slight, but I had a feeling it was that, that did most people in. I was not immune. "Do you want to stop?"

I thought about it for a good second, but *only* for a second. "No, not really."

"All right then."

She edged in to kiss me again but then pushed my head back with the palm of her hand. When I looked down, she was in the midst of doing away with my belt buckle, pulling down the zipper of my pants. My dick sprung out, engorged to the tip, and I let out a moan when she wrapped her lips around the head. She drunk all of me down in one try, her lips darkened and slick with saliva.

"Aw fuck," I mumbled as I started getting into it. I held her neck gently, guiding her mouth up and down the length of my cock until she came up for air rather abruptly. Still knelt in front of me, she whisked her bralette over her head, giving me a chance to admire her amazing tits.

They were perfect and natural, a rarity in Miami where the motto should have been *"Plastic Everything."* I licked my lips, taking her in as she put my dick in her mouth once more. "Oh god, that feels so good."

"Yeah?" she asked, stroking my cock up and down with her slippery hands. She positioned herself so my dick stood dead-center in between her breasts and seductively wrapped her tits around it, slowly moving up and down on my dick. Fuck.

I pulled her by the arms, willing her to stop. "Teddy, you look *too* fucking good doing that, but it's a surefire way to make me bust in, like, two seconds."

She laughed. "You say that like it's a bad thing."

"It's not that. It's just…that right there is all about me. I'd rather make it more about us. C'mere." She climbed onto my lap as I took one of her breasts in my hand, the other in my mouth. Her breath released in light pants as I took turns teasing her nipples with gentle pinches and soft flicks with my tongue. I wrapped my other arm around her waist and laid her down in the middle of the couch.

"Mmm, lay on your back, sexy. I wanna taste you."

So she did. I kneeled down in front of her, easing her shorts and panties off in one impatient pull. I licked two fingers and gently ran them down her sweet warmth, harder than I'd ever been with the thought of tasting her. She was waxed and smooth, and while it wasn't a preference to be bare, it made things easier when I wanted to get creative. Her pussy made me want to be nothing but creative.

My lips made contact with her thighs in feathery kisses and light licks until I couldn't wait any longer. I started slow, teasing to get a feel for what she could handle. Some girls were more sensitive than others, and I didn't want to overwhelm her with the pressure that came from my tongue ring.

"Mmm…you like that, sexy?" I flicked her clit with my tongue, spreading her pussy with my middle and index finger. It was so pretty, so pink, and she tasted so good, it encouraged my tongue to explore all over, from top to bottom, letting all of Teddy's juices coat the lower half of my face.

"Oh my god, Asher. I'm about to come…" she said as she pulled on my hair and tightened her thighs around my neck. I spread her legs apart and held them open, still licking, still sucking, wanting to see her beautiful body break down as she lost control of her nervous system. That wouldn't happen with her legs clamped around my neck.

She let out one last cry, her ribs rising and collapsing as she dragged out one last "fuck," pushing me away. I taunted her with one last lick and continued onto her legs. Teddy had some of the sexiest, shapeliest legs I'd ever touched. Everything from her thighs to her calves, even down to her feet, drove me insane.

"So you gonna let me fuck you?" I kissed her ankles and watched her squirm when I put her toes in my mouth. She pulled me by the collar of my shirt, assaulting me with primal kisses. Guess I got my answer. She grabbed my dick, stroking it in a way that felt good even without lubricant. I pulled my shirt off and slipped out of my pants, grabbing the lone condom I'd packed earlier, just in case. In unison, we let out moans of pleasure as my aching base invaded her warmth. I hooked my arms around her legs, testing out speeds and angles to find her breaking point, but this girl could take it all. Which was good because I had no intention of going easy on her.

She begged for me to go harder, deeper, faster, but once she broke out the pillow talk in Spanish, I was done. My muscles tensed as a rush of release traveled through my body like currents. Aw, man, that was nice. Here I was thinking the night was going to be a total waste.

There was a moment of awkwardness between us as we reached for our clothes and the closing credits to the movie scrolled down the TV screen.

"Look, umm…I don't know what happened just now, but if you want to just keep it between us…"

I turned around to find her curled up on the couch. Whether she'd actually fallen asleep that fast, I couldn't be sure, but I took that as my cue to leave.

There was a throw spread across the couch's back that I pulled off and covered her body with. I knelt down and caressed the side of her face with the crook of my finger. I felt sort of wrong leaving without saying goodbye. I leaned in to give her a soft kiss on the lips before whispering the words and seeing myself out.

CHAPTER THREE

Teddy

Groggy. Off-balance. Tired. I stretched out on the couch, snuggled in the throw I never used. All I needed was a second to orient myself. There was a lot to think about. Last night…

I didn't know what to make of last night. It was salacious. Insanely hot. Completely coincidental. The memory of all that took place flooded back to me. Asher's lips on my lips. Asher's lips on my breasts. Asher's lips on my…

What was I doing?

I bit my lip to the thought of Asher kissing me, touching me. Being inside me. Everything about him felt so good, but at the same time, so wrong. He was Reggie's friend. Repeating it in my head didn't help.

There were *some* feelings for Reggie. He was my friend, and I cared about him. Maybe there was even a point when what we had was something deeper, but he'd never wanted to take things past friends with benefits, and I wasn't about to breathe fire down his neck to get him to. Now that I was here, in the aftermath of sleeping with Asher, not being in a relationship was the only thing keeping my guilt at bay.

I'd made trouble for myself, but Reggie wasn't my boyfriend and made no plans to be. I kept thinking there was some bro code between them I'd just helped Asher break. Thinking about it now, I couldn't concentrate on much else. I remembered the way Asher's callused hands caressed and rubbed against my skin. How the barbell of his ring had felt massaging my tongue. The look in his eyes when…

I needed to stop. But I didn't want to. If I hadn't been at that billiards spot that night, I would've never seen Reggie. Then I would've never met Asher. I'd noticed him, noticing me. I'd even thought about him. But experiencing him was on a whole other level I wasn't ready for.

Ugh, it was time to get up and get this day over with.

The waiting room was empty today, which was how I liked it. I had my choice of what magazines I'd bring in with me to the treatment room should I get bored with my books and needed something light to glance at. I was early but sat in the waiting room for twelve minutes after my scheduled appointment before the nurse called me in.

I was sixteen when I'd first discovered a lump that had formed in the area near my underarm. It hadn't hurt and seemed far from serious at first, but the doctor in my father forced my hand. It wasn't long before I got it checked out. Turned out to be a swollen lymph node. Not great news. I had to have surgery to have it removed, but then the lymph node was sent to specialist, a pathologist or something like that. At the time, I thought it was so fucking dumb. Looking back now, if it hadn't been for those preliminary scans, I would've never learned I had Hodgkin's lymphoma, a cancer of the lymph nodes. Trust me when I say, it was a burden that's affected my life ever since.

There were three oncologists I had in my adulthood, and Volodymyr Zinchenko was always the one I was least excited to see. It was a cross between being with him for over six years and still not being able to pronounce his name and hating to hear bad news when it took double the effort to understand him to begin with. I nicknamed him Zinc. He didn't seem to mind when I called him that.

He'd become a distant friend of the family. Since my father was a prominent doctor in his earlier days, the same way Zinc was now, my father only trusted him to be my medical oncologist.

"Well, Theodora, here we are again."

"Yes, we are."

Zinc had a way of sounding condescending even when he wasn't trying to be, and it always pissed me off. He read well from me, that I didn't always deal with my Hodgkin's in the most constructive of ways. Thinking back to all the times he'd suggested counseling and therapy, but I was grateful when he'd stopped pressing the idea. One ear and out the other, that's where it always went.

I did eventually talk to people about it, but it was always unofficial and on my own time. It was only a few months ago that I'd joined a cancer survivor support group. I hated it at first, until I reached out to survivors in general and not my particular cancer. Sometimes it made me feel worse about myself, but there was always weed involved, so I dealt with it. Feeling bad about myself was worse than the cancer shrouded away in the vessel I called a body. So I tried to stay positive. Tried to stay fun. Tried to stay me. But anytime I did flap at the mouth, Zinc was like a singing parrot. He'd tell my parents if he worried about my mental state, and while my parents loved me, after my sister

Yenelisa's death, I didn't think they were strong enough to deal with any of this.

It was why I went through things myself. To my parents, healthy-me died long ago, and I didn't blame them for not wanting to remember me at my worst. I worked hard at trying to stay my best, but there were some things that were out of our control.

Two weeks ago I'd scheduled to meet Zinc for chemotherapy. Two weeks chemo, two weeks rest—only two months into my six months of mandatory chemo. I was *not* looking forward to it.

Against advisement, I lived in penguin cold caps during chemo treatments. I'd spent three years growing my hair out and keeping my roots thick so that last time I underwent chemo, my hair only thinned. The first round, I was completely bald, so when it grew back, I couldn't find a reason to relax my naturally kinky hair. It was such a blessing to have hair again that I told myself I'd accept it as it was. While they were excruciating to wear and expensive to rent, they let me hold onto my hair, and to me that was worth the risk.

Zinc thought it was vain, but it was hard convincing someone who was balding that you'd been through enough and just didn't want the questions, the stares, the obvious visible signs you had cancer.

After a round of small talk and the thousandth time Zinc went over the risks of my next chemo session, a part of me never knew what to do with the information that followed. Inability to conceive, which had prompted me to freeze my eggs long ago as advised by my mother. Peripheral neuropathy. Lymphedema. And countless other ordeals I might not be even aware of until the moment they presented themselves. For some reason, he always thought it was good to remind me that my eighty percent survival rate showed promise and that being a woman and under forty-five worked to my benefit. All I heard was my chance of dying was twenty percent higher than your average person. If you walked into a store and could only afford eighty percent of a life-and-death purchase, why did people think hearing that sounded comforting?

I didn't want to be here. I had to stay away from liquor but I wasn't always good at it. Sometimes I weighed the risks that came with it, but the first chance I got, I was definitely going to get stoned. At least it was less painful. Next on the agenda: finding someone to smoke with.

* * *

By the time a cab took me home, I had a mountain's worth of text messages. I only looked for the ones that told me what I wanted to hear.

Two from Noe.

Mi negrita, dimelo…

Oye, k hace?

One from Monica.

wyd

One from Reggie.

We should get up

Searching through my phone contacts, I group messaged a few people in the same thread.

Unofficial support meet?

Within minutes, my phone lit up with replies.

Racer: *Down*

Bridgette: *Can't make it*

Sol: *Wish I could come. Tucking in the kiddos*

Lucius: *Working. Definitely next time.*

Marta: *What time?*

Two people? That was good enough for me

* * *

Officially, if I didn't skip it, I met with a cancer support group on the first Saturday of every month. I preferred general cancer groups to those that catered only to Hodgkin's because the only people I ever encountered there were older men. We weren't all the same age, but the group was diverse enough to where we didn't need to all get along.

Unofficially, if our schedules permitted, we met up every once in a while to get high and be all about our feelings to each other with no one else listening.

Racer was fifteen and battling leukemia. Out of all of us, he was in the worst condition and the most passive about death. We were all going through shit, so none of us ever thought it fair to comfort him with lies that he might pull through and beat it. We all like to think we're strong enough, but his white blood count was low. Even for someone with leukemia. It seemed neither kind nor cruel to feed false hope.

He was a cool kid though. Claimed he was the envy of all his cousins with permission to smoke until his heart's content. For his sake, though, I hoped smoking weed wouldn't be the only thing he ever looked forward to. I was once there, feeling just as he did, but given more time to deal with it. I didn't feel sorry for him, just sad. The last thing any of us needed were people feeling sorry for us.

Marta was older. I never asked, but she looked to be at least in her forties. She'd survived breast cancer and had been cancer-free nearly twelve years, but the fear was always there, especially since it was a common killer on her maternal side. I was sure she was cute back in the day. Gender-fluid before there was a name for it. She had a son a bit younger than me, which always made me wonder what it was like to be a pregnant person who was in between genders. I'm sure in her time, no one even asked those kind of questions.

I was somewhere in the middle. Between hopeful and hopeless. Marta had kids, a career, and a bill of health twelve years long. I had neither. Maybe it's why I treasured this time so much. If no one else showed up, the two of them meeting with me reminded me the state of my mortality and that, outside of not struggling financially, I didn't have much to cherish. In less than ten minutes, I'd be too high to care.

CHAPTER FOUR

Asher

Work, work, work. Every day for the past eight days it'd been me, this cash office, and psycho customers making my life a living hell. Stupid questions about markups. Asking why particular items weren't in stock. It never occurs to people to ask about stuff when they were actually in the department. What the fuck did they expect me to do over in the front end?

Part of the reason I even became the cash office assistant manager was because I was good at telling customers what they wanted to hear. Sometimes I got faced with a person so difficult that I was able to see right through their bullshit. Those were the moments I lost my cool. Those were the moments that made the time drag.

A customer led me to a stacked bag of one hundred corn tortillas, pointing to the price they wanted it for, which was for another item at a third of the price.

"Okay, now that I'm over here, I see the pack of one hundred is clearly marked."

"Yeah, but everything is scattered everywhere. How can you tell what is what?" he argued.

"Easy, sir, by looking at the item count and matching it with the product. Like I just did. You saw what you wanted to see."

We argued to the point where I was ready to give him whatever he asked for at $1.99 just to get him out of my face. By the time we reached the cash register again, I just wanted him out of my life.

"Give it to him for the two dollars…"

"A dollar ninety-nine," he corrected me.

I faked a smile, walking the cashier through the overriding process, scanned my keycard and walked away. I left out the "Have a good day, sir" because why say what I didn't mean? There wasn't a better time than now to take my half, away from all the rush and commotion. As I made my way back to the produce section, I grabbed a bag of plantain chips, aloe vera juice, and a banana, waiting almost ten minutes in line to get checked out due to the long lines.

I had a little over nineteen minutes to chill outside, so I took a seat on the store's front curb and dove into my quick lunch. After work I'd be sure to hit up a real place to get some actual food in my stomach.

From a distance, the sound of a couple arguing echoed from the front of the store until it was right behind me. People were always screaming and yelling the first few days of the month, the store's busiest times, but it was mostly in Spanish and mostly about nothing. Just an argument full of a lot of "fuck you's" and "you ain't shit." And, of course, I had to be outside while it happened. So long to peace and quiet.

"I don't even know why I bothered driving all the way down here just to have you spew some stupid shit. Call me when you stop acting like an idiot!" a girl shouted on her way to her car.

Too furious to stop and look back, by her walk and BMW convertible, I knew it was Teddy. I watched her start her car and

Fast and Furious her way out of the parking lot. I turned around to see Reggie looking like he was ready to punch a wall or break some glass but thought better of it when a woman and her two kids walked by.

Without saying a word, he stomped back into the store, upset but not trying to get fired. Might be best to mind my business. I had no interest on hearing the ongoings of what those two argued about. All I knew was they weren't serious, but judging by that outburst, they sure did argue like they were.

A text from Teddy popped into my text threads.

Teddy: *Sorry didn't say hi...*

Me: *It's cool. Saw you were with Reggie. No biggie.*

A few minutes later, I got a text back from her.

Teddy: *You must think I stay worried about Reggie.*

I didn't have much time left on my break, so I didn't waste time texting back.

Me: *None of my business really. Only have a few minutes to text. Just letting you know.*

She waited another few minutes before I got another reply. I only had one minute to clock back in.

Teddy: *What time do you get off? I'll come get you...*

To tell myself I hadn't thought about her would be a lie. She'd been all I could think about for the past few days, but then again, the last time I'd heard from her was that night at the party. Wasn't sure what to make of that.

Me: *4:30. Meet me @ the Chase Bank on NE 18TH.*

She texted back a quick "*K*" just as I clocked in.

* * *

Teddy

I swear, I am *so* tired of Reggie. As much as we put each other through, there were just times I needed a timeout. Since my chemo a little more than a week ago, I'd been out of it for days, and right now, I didn't want to be bothered with someone who put me in a down mood. Cue in Asher.

Asher was something that should've gone wrong but turned out terribly right. Those gunmetal-blue eyes haunted me. No matter how long I'd gone in between denying it, I had to see him again.

There were a few hours before I had to pick him up, so I went home to take a quick shower and change into something more appropriate for the weather. Jeans and boots were too much for a day this hot, and my hair was already shrinking to my scalp as we spoke. I settled on a high bun, a tank top, and a flowy, floral mini-skirt in hopes I could beat the heat and still look cute. I think I looked cute.

When I pulled up to Chase Bank, Asher was taking money out of the ATM. He took longer than usual, so I sent him a quick *"Outside"* text that quickly prompted him to look over his shoulder to acknowledge that he saw me.

Asher: *Sorry. Depositing a check and transferring some money. Be right there...*

I could feel his eyes giving me the once-over as he sat down in the passenger seat, a small smile forming at his spider bite.

"You changed?"

His hand found its way to the top of my bare thighs, touching me in a way that had me worked up over nothing. He kissed my nearly naked shoulder making all the fine hairs on the back of my neck shoot up.

"You look nice," he said as he adjusted the seat to accommo-date his legs. "Hungry?"

At the moment I was, but not for anything you could order off a menu. "Sure."

"Cool. There's this spot in Little Havana someone was telling me about, but they don't speak English like that?" He formed almost as a question.

"Oh, so you want me to translate?" I teased.

"I know the bare minimum to get by, but it sure helps to have bilingual friends." As he read me off the address, and I programmed it into my car's GPS.

"Been living in Miami your entire life and only know the bare minimum. Shame on you, we have to teach you Spanish."

He smiled. "Only if you're my teacher."

I'd be his teacher all right. Too bad teaching him Spanish wasn't the first thing on my lesson plan.

* * *

"No tiene pollo? Puerco y carne de vaca, ya?" I asked after relaying what Asher wanted to the waiter.

"Ay si, mi amor, aqui tiene." He pointed to a chicken salad I wasn't at all interested in and then explained to me pork and beef were what people came here for, hence a menu with few chicken options.

"No te gusta la carne?"

"No, no, no, compay. Este... Estoy a dieta. Me entiendes?" Nosy ass. "Dame 'la carreta,' por favor."

"Okei, ya viene!" He took both of our menus and disappeared into the back.

"Are you really on a diet?" There goes that bare minimum.

"No, I just told him that. With Cubans, sometimes that's the only answer they accept when you tell them you prefer chicken. With one of my tias, until this day she calls me La Vegana because that's all I eat."

That and chicken seemed to be the only meat I could handle all week. It was best to keep it light. It meant less food I had to keep down from the nausea.

"So..." he started. He took a sip from his passion fruit milkshake and pierced me with those intense eyes. "What's up? What you been up to, Teddy?"

It wasn't exactly an ideal conversation starter to start with how sick I'd been over the past few days. Best to keep it light.

"Not much, can't complain. How about you?"

He shrugged. "Same here, I guess. You know how it is. Oh, I forgot to tell you." He pulled out a small paperback of one of my favorite authors, Nnedi Okorafor. It was one of her newer ones. Not my absolute favorite, but I did enjoy it.

"Turning you to the dark side. I love it. First step, Spanish. Second step, spec fic. Third? World domination. But only if I'm Brain and you're Pinky," I said at my weak attempt at a joke. How sweet was it that he actually cared about the stuff I liked? I wasn't friends with anyone who even liked reading. My mom used to tell me, *"Never trust a person who doesn't read. Your bisabuela learned at seventy-two. It's never too late."* But try convincing a generation obsessed with social networks and cell phones that. As you can see, my trust never went far.

"Not going to lie. It's some pretty heavy shit. I don't really read that much, but now I have questions. And I need recommendations." He laughed. He had the sexiest smile when he laughed.

"I have answers and I might have recommendations, but first thing's first. You have to get me hooked on something you like."

His lips curved to a slick grin. "Do you count?"

My eyebrows rose as I fought hard to bite back a smile. Nice one. "No, I do not count. Good answer, though. Next one you might want to say something I can actually take part in." The waiter came back with our food as I gave a quick thanks. Asher cut into his steak and took the first bite while I covered my salad in vinaigrette dressing and downed a forkful of spinach.

"Teddy, I'm simple. I like a lot of stuff."

"But tell me what you do regularly. Other than the obvious."

He rubbed his stubbly chin. "I like to skateboard."

Yeah, that wouldn't be happening anytime soon.

"I like basketball."

Okay, now we were getting somewhere. "What's your favorite team?"

"Oh, c'mon. Teddy, do you really have to ask? Heat, baby."

"Hey, had to ask. A lot of people left with Lebron. Just saying."

"I wouldn't have taken you for a basketball fan."

"I've been to a few games, but I wouldn't say I'm a fan. Just like the energy that comes with it. Everyone's always hype at basketball games. It's kind of cool."

He laughed. "Speaking of energy, a guilty pleasure of mine are those damn kid concerts. Y'know like *Dora the Explorer: Live* or, like, *Sesame Street on Ice* or shit like that. Before you go thinking I'm a borderline creep, I usually have a three-year-old niece present. Doesn't mean I can't enjoy it, too."

Trying to imagine Asher dancing around to *Blue's Clues* with a three-year-old girl was hilarious within itself. But also a little sweet. With all the tatts and piercings, it was first glance to read him as a bad boy, but I was digging the whole sensitive thing. If I hadn't been, I would've never given Reggie a second try. That guy was like Drake 2.0.

"Like I said before, I'm simple, Teddy. Give me video games, food, and good vibes, and you will never hear me complain."

Good because that was the last thing I needed in a friend right now. With everything that was going on, it was hard to hear people complain about superficial stuff. I'd give anything for a flat tire to be the biggest challenge I'd face this year. Dealing with something life-threatening definitely put your life into perspective. I couldn't be around people who made me feel bad all day. Reggie included.

"Hey, when you finish up your food, do you have someplace to be?"

He shook his head and continued eating. I knew just where we were headed to next.

* * *

Asher

It was cute how Teddy thought she could go toe-to-toe with me on the court in flip-flops and a mini-skirt. Poor girl looked like she was about to pass out. It was cool she didn't give up on the lesson though. She was a fighter. I had to give her props.

"Damn, I'm not wearing the right bra for this. That ball isn't the only thing bouncing up and down this court. My boobs hurt like hell right now," she said, guarding her breasts with her arms.

"My fault. You thought I was going to take it easy on you because you're a girl? I only go easy on the ones I don't think can hang with me. You've proven you can hang. You get me at my hardest… Okay, next time I may want to re-choose my words. That didn't come out like I planned it in my head," I said as we both held our stomachs from laughing so hard.

Teddy was easy to make laugh, and in the few times I'd seen her, I'd made it my mission to do so. We had a similar sense of humor. A big plus in my eyes.

"Mind if we sit over there?" she said, pointing to the playground nearby. There was a playhouse equipped with a slide, monkey bars, and a set of steps on both sides of it, as well as a merry-go-round a few feet away. My eyes fixed on the set of swings and I only agreed to sit if we could go a round on them. It was a childish pastime, but it brought me back to the time where I didn't worry about anything but how high I could go. Bills, work, and stress ate away at all those carefree thoughts, but every time I saw a swing set, I couldn't resist.

"These swings are friggin' low," I said, my feet touching the ground. Teddy was already halfway to the sky before I could even get going. Her feet swung to and fro until she no longer had to put force in to keep her momentum.

"I swear, I think we should switch or something. Seriously Teddy, my seat is lower than normal. Even for me."

"Your seat isn't too low. You're just not as good as me. You might be able to wipe the floor with me on the basketball court, but how is that height working for you now?" she teased.

I got up, and as soon as her swing propelled backward, I grabbed the chains of her swing to stop it.

"Get up, we're switching."

"Hell no! We're not switching. With your bitter behind. It doesn't matter where I swing, I'll still be higher."

"Okay, so if you'll still be higher, then let's switch."

She got up, jerking her arms back and forth like a bratty little kid and sat down on my swing.

"Holy crap, this is low. Damn, is this safe?" she asked as she adjusted in the seat, sitting far enough back that her legs dangled in the air. I was in flight, soaring like the birds in the sky, but even with a head start and a swing switch, Teddy still managed to swing higher, move faster, and murder me in our swing set race. She was right—she was better. But the idea of giving up without a fight did not compute.

"You win, you win," I declared in defeat. I was getting dizzy from the height and was in no rush to rid myself of what I had for dinner. She sighed and pivoting in my direction.

"I needed a day like this. Thank you for answering the call."

She got up and positioned herself in front of my swing. Couldn't help it. She was just…there. The compulsion to wrap my hands around her waist took over. I let my hands slip under her skirt and played with the string of the panties hugging her sexy hips.

"I love how your panties barely cover your ass."

"Boy, get off me," she joked, playfully pushing me back on the swing.

"C'mere." I pulled her by her arms, closer to me, giving in to the need to be closer to her.

It was supposed to be one time. Teddy was a friend of a friend, who happened to be *involved* with that friend. A new feeling, a new high, a new habit to add to a list of vices. Yet I couldn't get enough of her.

My clever hands found their way back to her panties, only this time I had more than the string in mind. I wanted what laid beneath those barely there V-strings. She moaned as my fingers drew shapes outside of her center and almost caved when they made contact with her slippery soft lips.

"Damn, Teddy, you're already wet," I said as my lips dragged across her stomach. With no one around, I was feeling adventurous. I wouldn't have minded taking her right here on this swing. My dick was already rock hard when it seemed like we had the same idea in mind. She helped me slide out of my pants, just low enough for a quick fix should someone stroll by. I slipped on a condom and watched as every inch of me got lost inside her hot stream of sweet desires. Her skirt was long enough to mask what we were doing from afar. Up close? We weren't fooling anyone.

She felt so good to be inside of. Even better that she knew how to get my blood flowing. She alternated between rocking back and forth and sinking up and down when she knew I was close, just to throw me off my rhythm. But I was loving it.

"Ride that cock, baby." I bit my lip every time she sunk back down. "That's it. Just like that," I whispered as I dipped her back to take me in deeper and give her thighs a rest. Her arms draped around my neck as she held tight, molding intimately against me, locking those dark eyes on mine. There was something in her eyes that drove me senseless. The craving, the mystery, the thirst in the way she looked at me, all made it hard to look away.

"Oh, shit, I think someone's coming!"

A guy walked his dog a few feet away as she hopped from on top of me, adjusting her skirt and panties as I struggled to pull my pants back up. We both shared a laugh about it before deciding to take a walk to cool down. "Well that was disappointing. But it still fun, though. I thought for a second, you were gonna come..."

"Fuck! I was close, too. But that swing seat was cutting into my ass anyway. Plus I'm mad visual. I have to have, like, tits, ass, something in my line of vision to remind me of what I'm doing. Next time, don't wear a bra," I joked. She pushed me off the walking trail into the grass, and I pretended to fall down hard on the ground.

"Oh my god, are you okay?" she said as she reached down to help me. I pulled her on top of me, masking her screams with my needy lips. My phone rang in my pocket, and I pulled it out, answering it before checking who it was. Reggie's voice poured through, talking too fast for me to register and too loud for me to hear what he was saying. There was a lot of stuff going on in the background. People yelling, an insane hip hop beat, and the occasional police siren. He must've been driving.

I motioned for Teddy to sit up as I tried hard to carry on the conversation.

"Listen," he was saying, "I need to go out tonight. These girls got me straight up suicidal. I just want to go out and get my mind off all these old numbers in my phone. Get my sights set on someone new, you feel me?"

I had a feeling this pertained to what happened between Reggie and Teddy earlier. As much as I tried to shield her from the words, she wasn't deaf. "Look, man, I'm not even around right now. I'm across town. Can't dude."

"It's not even for right now. I'm talking about later."

Teddy had no desire to listen to our conversation, and she excused herself to walk back to her car.

"What time were you trying to go out?"

He put me on hold for almost four minutes before he clicked back, updating his plans. "Tonight isn't good. Just got a call from my grams and turns out she needs her car tonight. What are you doing this Friday?"

Not willing to keep Teddy waiting, I told Reggie I'd let him know that day if I was down to roll. Things always changed the day of, so I couldn't give him a definite answer this second.

"We'll see each other at work. Just let me know then. Tired of all this mess girls put me through. I want to get my mind off things."

By *things*, I assumed he meant Teddy. I had no idea what the deal was between them, but I benefitted either way.

I hung up with Reggie and found my way back to Teddy's convertible. She was watching some YouTube comedy sketch on her phone in Spanish, so when she laughed, I had no clue what was so funny. I hopped in the passenger seat and caressed her chin with the crook of my finger, beckoning her to look my way. I figured I owed her some explanation to what she'd overheard with Reggie, but turns out she wasn't interested.

"Honestly, I don't care what he does. And I don't care what you do with him. That's your business. Besides, let him be with someone else. It's not like he's not doing that anyways. He's just pissed because he can't always have his way. Have fun, though. I never pass up the chance to have fun. I take it neither do you."

She was only half-right. I blew off a chance to party if I had better plans lined up. Right now, there wasn't anything going on better than this.

Between idiot drivers and rush hour traffic, it took her almost an hour to get back to our neck of the woods. I wasn't ready to call the day quits, but she insisted she had other things to do, which was somewhat convenient after my phone call with Reggie. She dropped me off in front of my house and left me with a lingering thought as I walked to my front door.

"Whenever you get a free second, call or text me. We could get up and have some more...*fun.*"

CHAPTER FIVE

Asher

Theodora_King is now following you.

The notification appeared across the top of my screen. By the time I clicked the activity page, it was lit with short comments and likes on Instagram. All from Theodora King.

She'd asked me to call her, but I hadn't. It's not like I didn't want to. I just hadn't gotten around to. Work this week made me tired and lazy, and I was no good to her on half a tank. I'd tried not to think about her these past few days. Her sexy lips. Her smoky eyes. Her creamy voice. Telling me to do things. Bad things. Bad things that felt so fucking good…

Stop!

Probably the thing I should've told myself both times before they happened. I thought I had more self-control. At least an *ounce* of loyalty. But questioning all that now didn't change what happened. It wasn't every day a girl like Teddy asked to chill, smoke, then hook-up. I was supposed to say no, but her body had convinced me otherwise.

The way that body felt…

Her skin was exactly as soft as I'd imagined it to be. Every part smooth to the touch. That night at her house, I should've left sooner. But I was a man of smoker etiquette. When someone offered their stash to you, it was rude not to chill. But hanging out got me into this mess. Into her mess. Into her.

I had to be careful. A guy like me might fall in love with a girl like her. That would be bad… I'd already made the one of the worst mistakes you can make, but at least she wasn't his girlfriend. That would've made things worse. Why did she have to be smoking hot? Or funny? Or so good at what we did?

To make matters worse, I let all these thoughts enter my head…at Reggie's house. He'd spent the last two hours at work convincing me to go to a club with him. Reggie required a wingman when he went out, but I had so much on my mind.

"All you have to do is make me look better to a few chicks. I'd even throw in a Starbucks gift card." Making Starbucks a factor made it worth some serious thought. I was all about the three S's: Starbucks, smoke, and sex. No particular order. I twirled the barbell at the center of my tongue. I only did it when I was thinking.

"Damn, Asher, you need the whole night to figure it out?"

"Dude, I'm thinking. Geez. All you said was no when it came to Vicki's party—"

"You didn't offer a Starbucks gift card," Reggie interrupted. It was rare for me, but I wasn't up for hitting clubs tonight. Too much on my mind. But I wasn't about to argue. My guilty conscience felt like it owed him something. "Fine. I'll go."

Reggie was a cool dude. He didn't act stupid getting dressed in front of me, even though he knew my tastes were open. I didn't like the label bisexual, but I wasn't gay and I wasn't straight. Believe it or not, you can be attracted to the same gender and not be attracted to every single person you encounter. Most straight guys I know wouldn't feel the same, but to each his own.

Reggie and me shared getting played in common, so it never mattered who it was by. But he was annoying as fuck when it came to his problem with women. Maybe it was a good thing I'd never heard of Teddy before we met. I'd talked him off of cliffs before with other girls. Maybe what went on between them wasn't as serious.

"Cool. So I'll have Neeko meet us at the door around eleven—"

I know he doesn't think he got away with that. "Oh, so Neeko's going?"

Reggie shot me a shrunken face before replying. "Yeah."

"So you don't need me there?" I asked, pointing to myself.

Reggie shot me another blank, rigid stare. "See, why you playing?"

"I'm just saying. Neeko's going to be there. What you need me there for?" Reggie was sneaky, but this was plain low. I wasn't the type to hold grudges, but Neeko? He was Reggie's friend. He burned his bridge with me the minute he borrowed money that he'd never paid back. Then, on top of it, pocketed my lighter. Unacceptable.

"You're still talking about that forty-five dollars, Ash?"

"Okay, let me borrow forty-five dollars from you." Reggie knew I was playing, but he wasn't about to fork it over. "All right then. I'm trying not to be petty, but it'd be hard not to ruin my night forcing myself to watch that motherfucker buy drinks, have fun, *breathe*, when he knows he owes me money." I tried not to sound upset, but our history with each other was tainted. "Plus, didn't he stop working for Diamond anyway?"

"He promotes at Sweat now."

"By Little Haiti?" Reggie nodded before stressing there'd be no dress code. "What's the cover?"

"Twenty-two," Reggie said with a bit of hesitation.

"Fuck you." I laughed, shaking my head. No way was I paying that to be a wingman.

"Damn, can a dude get his mind off things? You know I'd do it for you."

"Like you did with Vicki's party?" I snapped back.

"You know how it is with Vicki—"

"Vicky wasn't even worried about you. That back-and-forth at work? That girl is playing games. I saw her talking to twelve dudes that night. All that look better than you." That excuse Reggie tried to hide behind wasn't cutting it. "So don't flatter yourself, motherfucker."

"What if I throw in a twenty-five-dollar Starbucks card?" he said, making sure he stressed the amount. He was going to have to do better than that. His grams might as well be a professional online rewards system collector. I'd never seen a house filled with so many gift cards. It might've been an addiction, but she won them like they were currency.

"I can't hear you. Did you say fifty?" I coned my hand over my ear, emphasizing my point. Reggie threw his fists all over the place like a spoiled brat.

"All right! But you better amp it up. I'm talking asshole central. Make me look good as hell tonight."

* * *

I worked a night like this one of three ways. I was either the aggressive flirter, who never took no for an answer. If a girl was actually feeling that approach, I played up the jerk appeal that in turn made Reggie look like a gentleman. Tonight was easy. All I had to do was separate the girl from her friends. Preferred method out of the lot.

The hard part? Reggie always went for the prettiest girl in a group. He always had to make the time a challenge. It beat entertaining his whack-ass friend Neeko. I stopped myself twice from taking things outside. It was crazy how when people owed you money, everything they did rubbed you the wrong way.

I was nursing shot number three by the time Reggie approached me for the fourth time tonight. He wasn't having much luck with the last girl he pursued, and I was getting too drunk to be effective.

"Dude, what happened to Red Tank Top?"

"Red Tank Top took the drinks and bounced." At least she'd entertained him for a second. Reggie stuck out his neck and pouted, as if he'd expected a better outcome. It was why I never went for the hottest girl. I always went for the one most into me. Didn't always mean I was walking out with Naomi Campbell, but hey, my dick went home happy. Sometimes you needed to get laid.

I wanted a smoke, but as promised, I stuck around until Reggie didn't need my help. Nursing a cigarette between two fingers, it made its final resting place behind my ear before Reggie bumped into me. "What the fuck?"

"Don't look, but look." Reggie gestured over his shoulder to the opposite side of the room. He wasn't even clever with it, but I saw why he did. A girl in a white crop top and skirt navigated the bar. I thought he was about to make me play mediator, but then I caught a glimpse of who it was.

Teddy. We hadn't spoken since that day at the park, and I'd promised I'd call her but failed to do so. I wasn't sure how many lines I'd crossed, but I wasn't about to figure it out here. "Did you know she was going to be here?"

"Hell no. She's the whole reason I'm out right now. I'm trying to get my mind *off* her." Her eyes darted in our direction, and I had no idea what she was thinking. Would she think I'd rat her out? She didn't seem to give us much thought. She flipped her hair, took her drinks, and rejoined her party.

"Damn, she doesn't seem like she's worried about you." Or me. It was hard to tell since we were together. In all efforts to look less suspicious, my eyes shifted out of her direction. Figured if I stared too long, he would think something was up. Reggie, however, was feeling some kind of way. While he managed to convince me the whole way here he wanted a new girl to get hooked on that wasn't Teddy, it was clear he was feeling her. Hard.

"See this is the shit I was talking about. About how she get you hooked and then pulls away with no feasible explanation. Damn, she looks good." That we could agree on.

He went into this ten-minute monologue about how much fun he wasn't having—totally killing my vibe. Bitch-ass Neeko had us in VIP so there was absolutely no reason either one of us shouldn't be having fun.

Reggie shuffled on the sofa. "Come with me to the bar for a second."

"For what?"

"Are you my wingman or not?" Thinking it through, arguing with him wouldn't help my case. We made our way through the overcrowded club to the bar. The one advantage I had in a crowd was height. Never mattered whether I was stuck in the outskirts —it guaranteed I'd never lose a target and always caught the eye of the bartender. But Reggie had his sights set on Teddy. Horrible, horrible timing.

I was *supposed* to bump into her, pretending I hadn't noticed her in the swelling crowd. Reggie planned to catch up and just happen to run into her. *Right?* Like she was that stupid. It wasn't on my to-do list, but anything else would've brought up questions. Not a good look.

"Excuse you!" She'd been deep in conversation with her small group of people when I lightly nudged into her.

"My bad."

A look-over head to toe changed her entire demeanor. "Asher," was what her mouth read, but over the loud music and rowdy crowd, I only heard what she was willing to yell.

I bent over to speak directly in her ear. "What's good, Teddy?"

She was about to yell over the crowd, but instead gestured for me to bend over again to hear her better. "I haven't heard from you." Not what I expected her to say. I'd definitely been thinking about her. In fact, I couldn't stop thinking about her. But when I did, I remembered why I was here in the first place.

"Hey, Teddy," Reggie interrupted before I got a chance to respond to her statement.

She looked between us and wasn't buying it. "Guess I should've known *you'd* be here. What'd I see you, like, five minutes ago?"

Reggie gave a look over to her group. "You looked busy."

"I'm just here for a cousin's birthday. What are you two doing here?"

Reggie tripped over his words before leaning on an excuse Teddy wasn't buying. Had to give her credit for playing along, though.

She yelled over the crowd that she liked the sound of the music, despite trap not being something she listened to. She even swayed to it, despite the lack of space. Guess this was Reggie's chance. Probably wouldn't find a prettier girl than Teddy. I knew she wasn't his first choice, but leaving with someone was better than leaving with no one.

Should I be jealous? I'd only hooked up with her twice. It probably wouldn't matter if I were. They were flirting non-stop since they got to this point. So why did she keep eyeing me down, like she was waiting for me to say something? Maybe I was weighing them down. Seemed like a good time if any to get that smoke. "I'm going out for a smoke—"

Teddy grabbed my forearm, preventing me from leaving. "Take me with you! I need an excuse to get away from this party. No offense to my cousin, but this party is boring. I'm dying over here."

I didn't know what she was playing at, but it'd be awkward as hell to leave now. Me and Reggie were about to lead her to the VIP when Red Tank Top suddenly made a reappearance.

"Oh my god," she slurred in a drunken voice, collapsing in Reggie's arms. "I so want to dance right now. Don't tell me you're leaving."

"Girl, you're drunk."

She attempted to stand up straight, but failed miserably. "Am I?"

Those free drinks on Reggie must've been getting to her head, because she reached in to kiss him, which resulted in Teddy bursting out in laughter as Reggie pushed the girl off just enough not to disorient her. "Where are your friends?"

Red Tank Top shrugged. "I don't know. I can't find them." Reggie sighed so loud I heard it over the music. "Can you guys give me a minute? I'm not trying to be the reason this girl gets taken advantage of. I'll help her find her friends, but I'll be right back," he said as he helped the girl from tripping over herself.

I figured Teddy'd follow Reg, but she didn't seem interested in tagging along for the drama. She followed me to the VIP lounge and didn't hesitate to pull me over to the vacant couch.

"Just so you know," I told her, "homegirl's been playing him all night. Now she's playing games because she saw you with him—"

"Please, ain't nobody thinking about Reggie." She shooed my comment away as she took her shoes off. I didn't notice before, but her green nail polish contrasted against her outfit and skin, bringing the most attention to her toes. "My feet are killing me. I hate heels, but this place you can't wear sneakers."

I studied her foot, and it brought back memories of the first night with her. When I grabbed one, each one of her toes curled. "Damn, girl. You got some big-ass feet."

She smiled at me so wide it almost thinned out her full lips. "You weren't saying that the first time."

"I wasn't saying a lot of things the first time." Like *no*. Or *stop*. Or *please stop sucking my dick*. Even now I wanted to kiss her and her adorable feet. She pulled her foot away and placed both on the floor.

"You're not avoiding me now, are you?"

"Do I look like I'm avoiding you?" I asked defensively as she scooted in close to subtract the space between us.

"I didn't hear from you. Then I see you here tonight with Reg. I'm not stupid."

"I wasn't about to blow our spot. We literally fucked each other a few days ago. I'm still trying to make sense of shit." How was I supposed to know she'd be here and ready to address hooking up?

"It's okay if you thought it was a mistake. Doesn't mean I'm checking for you either. A *'we cool right?'* text would've sufficed."

"What makes you think I thought it was a mistake?"

"Asher, you are a hot mess."

"Maybe," I said with a smile.

She took out her phone and scrolled through a timeline of pictures. "If I show you something, promise not to laugh."

"I can't promise that shit." I shook my head, drowned in laughter before she even showed me anything. She handed over her phone, and it revealed pictures of her with a woman with the longest dreadlocks I'd ever seen. Glad I hadn't made that promise. "Why are you crying?"

"Because it's Nnedi Okorafor, stupid."

The name looked familiar. "Is that one of those authors you like?"

"Yes! Every time I've had a chance to meet her, I couldn't. And I was going through some serious shit when someone took that picture."

"That's dope."

She put her phone back in her bag. "I know you don't care, but I needed to brag to *someone*."

I put my hand to my chest. "Honored to be your bragging buddy."

She shook her head, hiding behind a laugh. "So outside of playing wingman—"

"Trust me. Not easy after…you know? But it brings up questions." I needed to defend myself. It didn't smell right to leave it that.

"What have you and Reggie been up to?"

"I'm not around the dude 24/7, Teddy."

That answer seemed to satisfy her, for a reason I didn't know why. "I don't know. In the few times I've seen you, two out of four times you've been together."

"What about that those times we *weren't* together," I teased. Teddy shot me a proud once-over. "But for real, this is unexpected for me. I'm only out because I felt I owed it to him after we…"

"You can say it."

"Since we hooked up." The world wasn't small, but I'd still ended up with the one girl I shouldn't have.

"Where do you normally go to have fun?"

I shrugged. "Raves mostly."

Teddy scrunched her nose and withdrew an inch away. "That might be a little too out my element. I doubt I'd look like anyone there"

"Teddy, there are tons of Black girls at raves. You might not like the music, but they're intense as fuck. Best when you're high."

She pointed to the crowd on the floor. "Is this not your normal scene?"

"I blend into every scene," I flirted back.

Teddy giggled, bit her lip, and scooched closer. "I was seriously butthurt I didn't hear back from you. Even if it's just to get up. I'm not going to be all on you like I'm your girl or anything. I'm not thinking about you like that anyway."

"I'm thinking about *you* like that," I said, shooting her a playful grin.

"I was just horny."

Destroying my bravado. "Figures."

She wrinkled her nose and furrowed her eyebrows like she was confused. "Excuse me?"

She was really going to make me say it. "Why even say it? You'll just act like you don't know shit."

"No. I want to know what you said."

I shook my head and psyched myself out. I knew I was decent-looking, but in the real world, Teddy'd be out my league just as much as Reggie's. "Like I have a fair shot with you anyways?"

Teddy's face turned into a scowl that only soured more when I didn't counter it. "Asher, you're so full of shit. I don't give the time of day to people I'm not attracted to, but all you have to do is burn me once."

"So if I would've texted you—" But she wouldn't let me finish.

"No. But if you want me to be someone who waits on you, I'm not that girl."

"All I'll say is you make me nervous. And I didn't have a lot of time to consider what I'd say if I did."

Teddy had those truth-bearing eyes. You didn't want her in your head, but she had the power to draw it out of you anyway. "I just like it when you're real with me. Like right now."

"What about you and Reggie?"

"I'm not talking about me and him. I'm talking about me and you." She sounded like she meant it. I was cool with staying friends. I'd never hung out with her with any ill intentions and wasn't entering a friendship expecting more. "Cool," I shot back.

She tousled her hair away from her shoulder and revealed a smile. "You don't have any cigarettes, do you?"

I reached in my pocket and grabbed my wallet. When my jeans weren't loose enough, I put loose cigarettes in a sandwich bag just in case the box wouldn't fit in my pocket.

"Want to join me? I saw an emergency exit near the bathroom. I'd go outside, but I'd get devoured out there."

"Sure. Give me a minute and I'll meet you there."

Teddy

That entire conversation required a ton of constraint. Asher put himself out there, but he had less to lose. If he knew an eighth of what he did to me, that'd be too much. At least I was good at hiding it. The games only started when someone knew you were into them. It was hard to get over on me. My poker face game was strong, and I could clear a deck before your cards were on the table.

I think a part of me still sort of liked Reggie, but the games? Not so much. I was thirsty if I gave *too* much attention, selfish if I didn't show enough. Even now, he was out there helping some chick he would've slept with if he hadn't run into me. We were by no means exclusive. He was free to do what he wanted. We didn't need to know each other's backlist. Especially since Asher became a part of mine.

Asher was messy, but I didn't mind getting a little messy sometimes.

I waited by the emergency exit until I saw Asher move through the crowd. I waved him over and disappeared inside. A squeaky open, and loud shut woke me out of my trace. I reached over and locked the door behind him. "You do realize I didn't get you in here for cigarettes, right?"

Asher nodded, smiling through squinted eyes. "I figured as much."

Asher closed the distance between us, leaning forward to

meet his lips to mine. I walked up two steps to match his height, so he wouldn't have to bend over, but he insisted it didn't bother him. Draping my arms around his shoulders, he boosted me up against stair railing.

He inched in for a kiss as he sucked and nibbled at my lower lip, our mouths formed to fit one another's in the most symmetrical of ways. Pulling away slightly, he gently knotted his tongue against mine, massaging the inside of my mouth with his piercing. I giggled, a hum vibrating between us.

His mouth traced against mine. "What?"

I laughed again. "You're just a good kisser."

He was. His lips weren't as full, but he knew how to use them. The spider bite on the right corner of his lip always seemed to add a chill to the warmth our mouths made. His lips gave one last long drag before he leaned out to look at me.

"What?"

He studied me deeply with discerning gunmetal-hued eyes. "If we're going to do this, when you're not feeling it anymore, just tell me. I don't want to get wrapped up in something I wasn't expecting."

I nodded. He didn't require more explanation than that before leaning back in to kiss me.

Between the lip-locking and petting, Asher pushed back my hair and kissed my neck, making me giddy like a schoolgirl.

"I want to tongue-fuck you so bad," he whispered in my ear.

"I'm not going to stop you," I flirted back between kisses, wrapping my arms around him. His hands reached under my skirt. I shivered at the feel of his callused hands on each side of my outer thighs.

My hands traced his facial hair as his own traveled deeper, getting caught in the string of my panties. Shit…I should've worn sexier underwear. Not expecting to see anyone tonight, I hadn't bothered wearing a matching bra. Not the best look.

Asher drew down the back of my panties until he pulled them

off completely. He knelt on a step below me, hiking my skirt above my thighs. His exploring tongue tasted the apex of my legs and nibbled the inside of my thighs. He didn't seem to care what my undergarments looked like—all he was fixated on was the reaction he got as he teased the slippery tip of his tongue to my outer lips.

A breath caught in my throat. He was teasing the shit out of me. I bit my lip, begging for his tongue. He spread his mouth back to my inner thighs, and I almost fainted. "Now you're playing with me."

His stare burned into mine as his mouth explored my skin. "I want you to tell me how you want it." Asher wasn't too proud to ask what I wanted, something I was more than happy to give.

"I want you to tease my lips open." Short of breath, I bit my bottom lip. Asher smiled and edged close enough for me to feel the warmth of his breath. His mouth kissed and licked my outer lips as his tongue slid between them, gliding its slickness against my clit. A light moan escaped me.

"Like that?"

As if he didn't know. I nodded and with a cracking voice said, "Exactly like that." He proceeded to work his tongue in an up and down motion underneath my clit. The pressure of his tongue ring added a different sensation that tickled, while the rest of his tongue teased.

"Do you like that?" he asked, interrupting the tension.

I licked my lips. "Fuck you, Ash. You know I do."

I spread my thighs a little wider to accept him, as I watched his tongue disappear and reappear, tasting me. I let my fingers tangle in his hair, getting lost in him pleasing me. Although the stair railing cut into the backs of my thighs, the velvety strokes of his tongue made me forget where we were. Tension built below my belt. I grit my teeth when his speed increased, forcing each one of my toes to curl upon impact. My thighs squeezed against his cheeks as the silence was replaced with my panting and swearing.

I wasn't sure how long I could hold out, so when he reached one of his hands underneath my bra to tease one of my nipples, a strained moan came out of nowhere, and a strong wave of spasms spread from my body to his mouth. My clit throbbed against his tongue as I held his face in it until my body was too sensitive to handle him. I pushed his face away from me, and Asher stood, wiping his mouth and chin of me.

"Damn, you're loud. I'm hard as shit."

I grabbed Asher's neck, beckoning him close for a kiss. His soft, wet lips tasted like me, only better. Because they tasted like him, too. My tongue traced the right side of his mouth, where his spider bite stood. He groaned, grabbing a healthy amount of my hips in his hand.

"What's wrong?" I said with a laugh.

"Nothing, that's just my sweet spot." He pulled out his wallet, picking out the only condom in his pocket, which he managed to slip on after pulling himself out of his jeans. I reached down to rub his cock and help him guide it inside me until you couldn't see where his body started and my body ended.

The angle was awkward—balancing my weight on the railing, while my body closed in over his cock, clenching him with every thrust. He held my thighs apart, watching himself slip in and out of me, with a slack-jawed expression on his face. He bit his lip, grunting and thrusting inside my inviting warmth.

"Teddy, you're seriously wet as fuck."

Could you blame me? Asher was modest, but he had the pussy-eating skills of a god. I leaned upright, attempting to gain my footing on the railing. Asher pulled out of me, reached in for a kiss, and whispered for me to turn around. Stepping off the railing was a relief—the backs of my thighs couldn't take it much longer. I pressed my back against Ash as his busy hands pushed my skirt up higher. He eased into me, making us both moan over the friction.

Asher brought his hips to my backside in slow, long, deep-plunging strokes. I'd already orgasmed, but the way he filled my body made my knees weak and my thighs tremble with each new thrust. He continued a steady speed that made my body clench down every time my body reaccepted him.

"That feels so good, Ash." Because I thought he should know.

He increased his speed, grabbing hold of my hips. "Do you like that?"

Instead of slow, controlled thrusts, his body now entered me in faster, penetrating pounds. He leaned over to kiss my neck up to my ear, but I'm sure it was only to whisper sweet nothings of how horny I made him, how sexy he found me, and how good I felt to him. His pace only slowed as his lips enraptured mine in an upside-down kiss.

It was time for him to fuck me like he meant it. Asher arched in close, dragging his hands over my breasts, until my bra barely covered any part of them. With his mouth so close to my ear, I held his face in my hand, accepting each frenzied thrust. An exchange of dirty talk between us ended in shared swears and cracked moans of pleasure. Telling him to come for me was all his body needed to lose control.

He plunged three hard thrusts into me, and his tight grip enveloped me into an embrace. His damp face was drenched in sweat as I turned to accept his willing lips. He finally withdrew from me, and his zipper and belt were nearly secure by the time I pulled down my skirt.

"That was intense." Asher lit his cigarette from earlier.

"Can I get a drag?"

Asher nodded, handing it over. Better to smell like cigarettes than sex. I handed it back to him as he puffed a few more drags, tossed it on the floor, and stepped on it to kill the fire. He edged toward the emergency exit, about to leave, before I pulled him back.

"You were about to leave without kissing me. That is unacceptable."

He arched an eyebrow with an unreadable smirk and met his lips to mine. After three more back-and-forths, we mutually agreed to cool it for the night. I pushed him toward the door, and he laughed, unlocking it. I thought it might be best to wait a few, just in case someone was by the door. I took the time to freshen up with a few spare baby wipes I left in my bag, discarding them in a waste bail in the hallway.

Being preoccupied, I hadn't checked my phone in all the chaos.

Are you avoiding me?

I wish this fool would stop texting me.

Session soon?

Did I feel like it? I'd never turn down a chance for a smoke, and it'd been awhile but…

Where'd you go? Meet up later? Reggie.

Funny how he wasn't that concerned when my attention actually was his. I started a reply, but thought against it. It wasn't my intention to make anyone sweat, but I never got to anyone's reply right away. I wasn't about to start now.

CHAPTER SIX

Asher

How the hell was I here again? I knew what'd happened. I'd definitely felt what'd happened. I wasn't likely to *forget* what happened. Yet here I was, in the very situation I'd meant to prevent.

Maybe if hooking up with Teddy had only gone down once, I could've worked harder to make it a distant memory. Shit, even after the second time, I could've buried it onto the of *"The people I shouldn't have slept with"* list.

However, I was beginning to think neither of us would ever practice self-control around one another, or at least didn't want to.

I contemplated the first time I'd met Teddy, and how it lead back to now. The sole reason I shouldn't have hooked up with her, was the reason I'd met her in the first place.

Reggie.

Why was the girl I shouldn't have been with, so perfect for me?

Teddy had something about her that made every nerve in my

body come alive. You couldn't come down from her if you wanted to—but if you were anything like me? You fucking loved it.

I never expected the benign with Teddy. That girl kept you on your toes at all times. She should've been a handful, but I could keep up. The problem with keeping up?

I wasn't the only one into her.

Maybe *into* was overselling it. My boy, Reggie, had history with her. In the times I'd known what their story was together, it seemed they actually were history. They'd never been in it on a serious level.

I had my own measuring stick when it came to loyalty, and the only thing I'd been sure about was that I'd overstepped my boundaries. The dog in me, though? So long as she pursued me, I wasn't likely to quit. I wanted more of her, and wanted to give her more of me.

So much more. I'm talking break-that-back more.

By the end of the night, she was nowhere to be found. Reggie seemed to have his hands full helping that girl find her friends, so I didn't bother sticking around after we parted. A taxi seemed easier than being inches away in a passenger seat knowing my skin, my scent, my taste all had remnants of Teddy on them.

* * *

The level of energy I had today, man. I'd gotten a decent six hours before it was time for my shift to start. I'd be too busy to do more than work, but I had that foreboding feeling that I'd eventually encounter a questioning Reggie.

I didn't want to think about him. Not when all my mind could do was think about Teddy. She was so ingrained in my mind, I couldn't even take a shower this morning, without jacking off to her face.

Or her legs wrapped around my hips. Or her lips wrapped

around my length. Those eyes of hers, they had their way of melting every defense I had. It just sucked big time that there might come a time where this thing between us would have to end.

There was no way of getting around Reggie not finding out for long. I wasn't the kiss and tell type, so the only way he'd find out was if she slipped up. But I had a feeling she was good at conveying she hadn't just slept with someone. I mean, we'd gotten this far.

Maybe after a night of sleeping things off, I'd be a rearview regret. Wasn't likely though, since she definitely wasn't mine.

The likelihood of running into Reg was high. We did work together, after all. I just wasn't looking forward to—nor was I prepared for, what I'd say if he asked how my night went.

I wouldn't lie so much, as withholding the truth. But I'd have to come up with something. For now I was thinking too much into it.

Fortunately, it was a hectic day at work. PriceSlash was a discount grocer that was always busy as hell. District managers never approved hours on weeks that didn't fall within the first two weeks of every month. We did our best the first week of each month, but the momentum often kept up during the week, too.

What we didn't plan for, were the random days at the end of the month, where we weren't allowed to schedule a lot, but encouraged to call in cashiers when needed. Fat chance when you gave them four days off in a row. All that time, they're out looking for better jobs.

Front end was the worst with call outs, call-ins and turnover, and in a place like this, even managers weren't immune to ringing.

I'd started as a cashier, but I was relieved for each promotion that got me closer to being as far from cash lanes as possible. PriceSlash claimed it kept its prices so low due to hiring less help, and having customers bag their own groceries. In hindsight, it *sounds* like an easy as hell job. But my back wasn't having it. Placing items of the belt, while in turn returning it to their carts required a lot of bending forward. Needless to say, these registers weren't built for someone over 5'6". Slowly I'd worked my way up to a supervisor, to an assistant manager to the cash office.

The hours still sucked, but I actually got them if that meant anything. We only had two cashiers scheduled, so it required one of the supervisors—Deana, my homegirl and myself to keep the lines down. Did I forget that was in addition to the cash office responsibilities, as well as handling customers and FE as well?

I suppose there was one plus.

I'd seen Reggie, but we never had time to talk. Not to say he had intention to. Even if he did, who knows what he'd bring up or where the conversation might start. But I didn't plan on bringing it up. Figured the less I knew and shared, the better.

That race to the time clock? Not quick enough.

"You looked like you had your work cut out for you today." Reggie quipped. His body language read far from suspicious, but I'd only know more from talking longer.

"You know how it is up front. I'm about to transfer over to produce so I can do your job. *Nothing*." I stuck out my tongue, bold like I usually was. It'd only betray my position more if I acted dumb or quiet.

"That's why it took six hours for that first break." Reggie taunted. I reached in and hit him, followed by a "Man, fuck you." It seemed better to bring attention to last night than avoid it, so I didn't hesitate to ask how the night went. "So how'd you make out yesterday?"

Reggie made a hissing noise with his mouth, before swatting the air in front of him, as if it were meant for a person.

"That bad, huh?"

"Let's just say, I'm glad to be single."

I listened in, punching my employee numbers into the time clock, in attempt to look like I was paying attention but not all there. Typical rants and raves. People playing games. By people, I assumed who he really meant was Teddy. Night ruined playing knight in shining armor, helping that girl find her friends.

I lectured him on why *Red Tank Top* had been a bad choice. Sure she'd been prettier than some of her friends, but there'd been a girl in the group straight eye-fucking Reg. She'd been a lot less drunk and a lot more ready. Guess it didn't concern him either way once Teddy came along.

Even if she'd been his intention, he made sure to put extra emphasis that he wasn't thinking about *any* girl, especially Teddy. Which was funny—she was all *I* could think about.

To be honest, I didn't know much about Theodora. What I knew, I liked. She was a bit of a low-key dork on the low. For the record, that was incredibly sexy. It was fun when you didn't have everything in common with a person. Sharing all common interests meant you'd only ever do the same shit, and I didn't have to necessarily like something to do it.

I'd never been big on school. I didn't go to college out of high school, and my tattoos made it hard for people to see me in a professional environment. But reading wasn't as bad when you had recommendations.

I wasn't going to be up her ass unless she wanted me there, though. But out of the five most used phone numbers I texted in my phone, she was the one whose messages I anticipated the most.

CHAPTER SEVEN

Teddy

Ugh. It was one of those Netflix kind of nights, sans the come-over-and-chill part. My mind was in so many places, I needed the time away. I needed to be numb, but reruns of *Glee* would have to do. Couldn't think of a more numbing experience than watching anything from Fox.

Me: *Sup*

Asher: *NM. Hbu*

A text session with Asher was always a lot of back and forth. No one ever texted me as often as he did, once the thread got started. It wasn't always about getting up. Sometimes he'd just send shelfies from brick-and-mortar stores, asking whether I'd heard of something. I adored that, but what I really wanted was to see him again.

Me: *What do you do when you're out by yourself?*

Asher: *Idk*

Me: *Don't you go to raves?*

Asher: *Yeah*

Me: *What do you do there?*

Asher: *X. Shrooms. LSD.*

Ecstasy was okay. I liked that it made me feel horny, but the long-term effects weren't worth it. I didn't know much about the other stuff. Weed was my drug of choice. Nothing else worked for pain better than that.

Me: *What's LSD like?*

Asher: *Better than sex*

Me: *Now I have to try it*

I waited a second but didn't get an immediate response. I took out a bottle of polish and proceeded to paint my toenails a burgundy red, knowing that would keep me busy as I waited for a reply. My phone vibrated, but I gave myself a minute or two to finish.

Asher: *It's trippy. Lasts longer than weed. Better to be with someone if you've never done it.*

Damn. Seemed heavy duty.

Me: *Yolo*

Asher: *You're funny.*

Me: *Just waiting for you to invite me ;p*

Asher: *Ha. What are you doing Tuesday?*

* * *

Asher

Miami was strange in a way where you could go from the suburbs to the rougher side of town in a ten-minute drive. I lived in what was left of Little San Juan. Between all the money-hungry investors and developers, wouldn't be long until it started housing cupcake shops and a whole lot of other shit only hipsters liked. But Teddy—she was on the wealthier side of Edgewater. I'm talking, the view-from-her-room-had-you-staring-at-the-water wealthy.

I rang her doorbell, waiting while she buzzed me in and warned me to take the staircase because the elevator wasn't working. By the time I got to her apartment door, I was convinced she wasn't the least bit interested in getting high. My eyes folded over the tank and shorts she'd managed to fit every curve of hers around.

"Damn, girl, are you trying to give me a heart attack?"

She jabbed me in the shoulder and burst into laughter the moment she looked down at my shoes. "Boy, I know you are not wearing Toms."

I adjusted my hat, hiding behind a playful smirk. "Damn, what do you have against Toms? These shits are comfortable."

Teddy laughed, but not before telling me I was corny. "Did you want to watch something beforehand?" she asked.

Following her to the couch, I did my best to explain some of the grittier details of an acid trip. "We can, but since it's your first time, I wouldn't suggest it. You didn't eat anything, right?"

She nodded. "Can we have sex on it?"

I loved where her mind went. "Let's just see if you like it first. It's a little different than being high on weed and takes a lot longer to come down from. So is it cool if I crash until I'm cool?"

Teddy nodded as we got comfortable on the floor. I pulled out the sheet wrapped in paper towel and ripped off about 200ug for both of us. It was hard to know the exact potency per dot, but on the safe side, less was more.

She lifted up her tongue to accept the dot, prompting me to do the same. Forty-five minutes in, I was already seeing things clearer and more pronounced than they were. Even Teddy's breathing sounded louder to me. I'd managed to pin her to floor, spending the bulk of my time kissing her neck, shoulders, and chest.

"You smell so good. I just want to keep kissing you."

A small giggle left her, made louder by the trip. I leaned up to look her in the eye. They were so dark they usually looked black, but on a trip, it was like the white in her eyes made the dark brown seem more like her skin color. She reached up to run her fingers through my hair, something I was a sucker for even when I was sober. I bent down to kiss her again and didn't fight it when she scrambled to climb on top of me.

"It feels like I'm swimming in your eyes," Teddy joked, reaching for another kiss. She licked my neck, a slippery sensation made razor-hot by the trip. "You taste like ice cream."

She giggled again, so I knew she was reaching the trip's peak quicker than I was. I knew damn well I didn't taste like ice cream. She held her arms out, like she was flying, and asked me not to let go until she felt safe on the ground.

When I reached in to kiss her neck, she went into a giggle-fit, adding that my lips felt like a pillow fight.

"You would care if I died right?"

The sentence echoed throughout my eardrum, like a broken record that wouldn't stop playing. For little to have led to it, it was an intense-ass question.

"Yeah," I answered back. "Where is that coming from?"

She wrestled and managed to crawl off me. I was reaching my trip's height but still coherent enough to understand or interpret anything she said. She tried to hide between the loveseat and the nesting table left of the couch. By the time I crawled on top of her, she was already crying.

"I don't want to die," she kept repeating to herself.

"You're not going to," I said, trying to comfort her. Whatever was running through her head affected her trip. The high made you feel amazing when you felt good, but it didn't do so well the other way around.

"Yes, I am. I don't want to die. I don't want to think. I just want to feel."

I'd never seen Teddy so vulnerable. "You're just getting scared. I'll make you feel better."

I crawled down to her waist. My vision was functional, but my arms kept getting tangled in her legs. I could never figure my limbs from someone else's on a trip. One thing to remember:

Teddy=brown; me=pale as fuck. Her panties were a setback as each polka dot jumped out at me, poking me in the eye. Her body seemed so far away that it was like diving into water and trying to anticipate the drop. When the sound of a cell phone rang across the room, she screamed, rolling over to cover her face. Now didn't seem like a good time for oral sex.

"I'm going to help you to your room." She'd never be able to sleep this wired, but familiarity was the only thing to make things more comfortable this zoned out.

I must've watched too many Spike Lee movies at her place because it felt like a fucking dolly shot from the floor to her bedroom. She slumped onto the bed and pulled hard on my wrist when she thought I was leaving.

"Please don't leave me."

It was bad etiquette to leave, so I'd already planned on staying. She pulled my arms to wrap around her as she sunk into me, like we were one person.

Sometimes a friendship got deeper during an acid trip. I wasn't sure how it'd affect me and Teddy, but as long as I was keeping her company, there could've been worse ways to end a trip.

* * *

It was past ten by the time I came to. My system was still anxious, but it wasn't anything I hadn't dealt with. The last five hours were a blur. There were worse places to wake up than the middle of Teddy's living room floor. I had until noon to be to work on time, so I went on a scavenger hunt to gather everything I came with.

She jumped at the sight of me when she walked out her room, a clear sign she wasn't expecting me. "Holy shit, you're still here?"

Turns out, I was more sensitive to sound than I realized. Her voice echoed in my eardrums, like she was speaking from a microphone. "I must've went to sleep. I don't remember shit, but I'm not tired so I guess I did. You okay?"

She shrugged, unconvincing. It was a lie to say I didn't remember *anything*. Some of the shit she'd said on her trip was hard to forget. "Said some pretty trippy shit last night."

Teddy sat on her couch. I wasn't sure if she was trying to hide her expression or whether rubbing her face was genuine, but it seemed off. "Like what?" she asked nonchalantly.

I sat on the arm of the couch with enough distance between us to have my guard up, but close enough to study her reaction, if she'd even have one. "I don't know. Just some shit about you not wanting to die and shit. It sounded totally left field, but as your LSD mentor, I figured I'd ask just to make sure there wasn't anything wrong." I laughed, attempting to make a joke from it. "What was that all about?" I tried again before the moment was lost.

She stood her ground, pointing her finger to her chest like I was accusing her of something. "You're really going to ask me about some stupid shit I said when I was high?"

I countered with my own defensive stance, holding my hands out to resist the change in mood. "Whoa! I was just asking if you were okay. It freaked me out, but from your reaction, you seem fine. It's not that serious. You act like you saw a Nicholas Cage movie or something."

Teddy shook her head and stood. "You need to go."

"I was just kidding."

"Well, I wasn't."

That was…harsh. I hadn't pegged her for a Nicholas Cage fan, unless it was something else. I wasn't about to find out. She roamed to her kitchen, soundless, waiting for me to take my stuff and leave. I stalked away, leaving in a huff. Guess I shouldn't count on hanging with her anytime soon.

CHAPTER EIGHT

Teddy

I'd been off the grid for a few weeks due to some trippy chemo sessions. There was a combination of different treatments my oncologist drew up for me and a collection of pills I was trying for the first time. Personally, they made me feel the worst I'd ever felt. Most of my support group were more supportive than the people I knew outside of them, so once in a while one of them would check on me. My papi every so often sent an associate of his to drive me to appointments when I couldn't get there and back myself, but other than that, I barely had the energy to move.

When I felt at sixty percent, which to me was better than zero, I wanted to get my mind on something else. What I wanted to do was get up with Asher, but the last time we'd spoken, it had been too much for me to handle.

I'd had some bad experiences with harder substances before, but that night guaranteed I'd never go anywhere near another hallucinogen. That stuff made nightmares come alive, and I wasn't happy with myself for sharing my darkest fear with a guy I was yet to fully know. How could I ever face him again?

Anytime I was fresh from a week of chemo, my text threads looked crazy. Quite often they were never my concern when I was feeling this sick, so I always came back to close to one hundred messages. Maybe more. This time wasn't any different. Out of the three weeks I'd been AWOL, Asher had only texted me twice.

Asher: *My bad, Teddy. Want you to know I'm sorry*

Asher: *Not gonna blow your phone up. Just wondering if you were okay...*

At least he cared. I mean, at least I think he did. While they weren't the kinds of messages I'd been hoping for, I chose not to delete them. Just as a reminder.

There were over thirty from Reggie. All ranging in the typical messages I'd expect from him.

Reggie: *What's good?*

Reggie: *Tryin' to get up?*

Reggie: *Got a taste for Starbucks...*

Reggie: *Why you playin'?*

I deleted all the new ones except for an old" *Smoke?*" text. The only one I had any interest in at the moment. Getting smoked out. I texted him back.

Me: *What you got?*

It took him a few minutes to text me about some weak strain I'd never even heard of, but fuck it. My dealer was away, and I needed to get out of this house and get my mind clear. He texted.

Reggie: *Come scoop me up.*

I shot him a reply.

Me: *No dice. Swing by yours instead?*

Reggie: *Sure*

Me: *OMW*

I pocketed my keys and made my way over to Reggie's side of town. He may not have been the one I wanted to spend my time with, but until I found the courage to confront Asher again, a familiar face would have to do.

* * *

Every time I hung out at Reggie's house, I instantly regret it the second I stepped foot inside. He lived in the basement of his grandmother's house, which would have been all right if the woman didn't hate my guts. But like every momma's boy or grandma's boy or whatever the hell he was to her, one look at me and she'd decided she didn't and never would like me.

Whether it was my car (apparently I was bougie) or the way I dressed or even the fact that, no matter how rude she was to me, I treated her with respect—she hated me. Claimed I was a fake hussy. Which I guess was sort of true since I wasn't her biggest fan, but when I was in her house, I kept my mouth shut. I had some sense, but it was why I never chilled here.

He laid down on his bed and signaled for me to come over, which I did. But if we weren't smoking, I couldn't think of a thing I wanted to do on his bed.

"C'mere, Teddy."

I scooted in a few inches closer, yet not close enough to wipe the agitated look off his face.

"Ugh, Teddy, what's the matter? I thought you came over to chill."

"No, Reggie. I came over to smoke, but being how your grandmother's here, I don't see that happening. Did you even have any weed?" All signs pointed to no. Often if he was down for a session, I was the supplier.

"Look, Teddy, I just told you that to get you over here. Now that you're here, I wanted to talk to you about something I've wanted to bring up for a while."

Sigh. I did not come over here for some serious talk. He leaned up on the bed, adjusting his dreads in a high ponytail. There was a time where I'd gone nuts over an insignificant gesture like that, but now all I could set my mind on were spider bites, sly smiles, and a certain pair of gunmetal-blue eyes staring back at me. A lot of talk for a girl who was too embarrassed to contact the guy.

"Look, Teddy, I don't even know how many times we've had this conversation, but right now I really just want you to hear me."

I gestured with my hands for him to spit it out. Not sure where it would lead, but he needed to get on with it.

"How long have we been talking to one another?"

I shrugged. "Well, we've known each other five months, give or take. Do you want to count the *whole* friendship?"

"Okay, see, that's what I wanted to talk to you about. This whole cat-and-mouse thing. I want to be done with this. I know you and I aren't exactly just 'with' each other, but what if I was trying to be?"

Okay, so here was the rundown of me and Reggie. We were friends. We'd met a little over five months ago, and there'd been a time it was me on the other end of this conversation. I'm not the kind of girl to fall for just anyone just because we'd have a few successful sessions in bed and a few similar interests, but Reggie made me laugh, something I really valued in a partner.

The first two months of our friendship were magic. Nothing but smiles, giggles, and cute memories to this day. It wasn't as if I'd put the idea to get engaged in his head, but I'd been interested in being more than what we were. I put so *few* offers out there, so I thought by voicing how I felt, the attention I craved would get matched up. But boy, oh, boy, was I wrong.

Since then, I liked being around Reggie. Not having many friends these days, I was holding onto whatever we had, but the feeling for something serious was gone. Once I knew he was only interested in casual, that's all I ever called him for, and now because I wasn't giving him the attention like in the beginning, he wanted me all the time. Figures.

"Reggie, what did you tell me like a few months ago? That you didn't have 'time' to entertain being more than just friends. Isn't that what you said?" It was always one thing or another with him.

"Teddy, you of all people know how pessimistic I am. And you stay on that bullshit. I'm always afraid to invest the time, because you're always 'Call me, don't call' all the time. I know it sounds messed up but sometimes it's easier to mess with girls who aren't as cute or confident as you. It's fucked up, but that's just how it is."

I rolled my eyes. Was I really entertaining this garbage?

"It's like when I go to sleep, all I do is think about you. I wake up, and my first thought is of you. Maybe I could have come to this conclusion sooner, but I wasn't trying to get my feelings hurt."

Take in mind, while he was saying all this stuff, his eyes and hands were glued to his phone, not paying me any mind. It didn't matter what we were ever talking about, Reggie was obsessed with the phone at his fingertips. If nothing annoyed me more than life itself, it was that. Whatever his cell screen provided, it was more important than me.

"Okay, so are you finito? Or can I go next?"

He shook his head back and forth, annoyed, phone still in hand, never breaking away to look at me.

"Okay, so here's the deal. Reggie, I like you—"

He cut me off. "Okay?" he faced his palms out and shrugged.

"Would you let me finish? So that's the deal. I really like you." I took a long pause, which caused him to finally look up at me, away from his screen.

"So what's the problem?"

"The problem is I don't get everything I need from you, and before you go thinking it's about money or something else super-ficial, allow me to demonstrate what I mean." I took his phone from his prying hands only to have it quickly snatched back from me. You see, the problem weren't the dozen girls in his phone—

what I cared about was something I never had from him from the start.

"So half the time I've been here, you haven't stopped looking at your phone. You say you want to be with me, but I don't even have your undivided attention. Second—" Because there was always a second or a third or a fourth with him. It never stopped at just one. I pulled out my phone to sift through the thread full of texts he sent me. I read them aloud.

"'Hey, Teddy, you tryin' to smoke?' 'Hey, Teddy, you think you could give me a lift from work?' 'Hey, Teddy, you tryin' to get Starbucks?' I don't have one message from you that says, 'Good morning, beautiful.' Or, 'How was your day, Ted?' 'Ya know I haven't seen you in a while, Teddy. I think I kinda miss you.' It's always, how much can I ask Teddy for today?"

He frowned. "Teddy, it's not even like that and you know it."

"No, Reggie. I don't know a damn thing."

"Teddy, look. I'm a guy. Not every way I express myself is going to be romantic enough for you or emotional enough for you. Guys…we're just not built like that—"

And now was the time I had to cut him off because he was talking nonsense.

"It's funny how you should say that because this new guy I've been dealing with is *exactly* like that. Last time I checked, he was a guy."

The second it left my mouth, I wished I'd never said it. Sure it was a known thing that Reggie and I saw other people, but we never talked about them with each other. Never ruined the moment by providing the details of who we saw that weren't each other. To make it worse, since I'd started sleeping with Asher, I'd completely cut Reggie off.

Not because I didn't have good sex with Reggie—I did—but with Asher, I had *great* sex. It was hard to downgrade from a mind-blowing situation.

"So who's this new guy? What's homeboy's name? Are you guys serious?"

All questions I didn't have answers to. Were we serious? Far from it, but I would give anything to be anywhere he was, than where I was right now. Reggie with his million and one questions.

"Reg, it doesn't matter who he is. You told me months ago that you didn't have time. Clearly that hasn't changed, and you're not going to find time out of nowhere. Your friendship..." I thought long and hard on how I wanted to close this statement. "As much as I hate to admit it, your friendship is important to me. Let's not fuck it up by adding things in the mix that don't blend well."

The stairs creaked as his grandmother walked painfully slow down the staircase. She carried a basket of clothes close to her right side, which I assumed she'd planned to clean. That's how it always was whenever I came over. She was always trying to find an excuse to be nosy. Doing laundry was the easy since the basement was home to the house's washer and dryer, but I could pretty much count on her to wash clothes if I was over here for longer than she wanted me to be.

She moved at a snail's pace, sorting out her laundry, and as she started her load, it became obvious that she was going to stand there until I left. The way this night was going, I was in no real mood to be there. Grandma did me a favor.

"Well, Reg. It's getting late. Best to get going." I hopped off his bed and ignored the kiss he leaned in to give me. I wished his grandmother a goodbye as I made my way out. I got to my car and took out my phone to send my favorite group a mass text.

Me: *Unofficial meet up?*

The first one to text back was Racer.

Racer: *Count me in*

CHAPTER NINE

Asher

I was in dire need of a haircut. The grown-in sides made the undercut non-existent, and that was *not* the look I was going for. I'd do it myself, but the mirror in the bathroom wasn't high enough to get a good look without sitting. I only trusted one barber with my hair. It required being up before noon, which almost never happened on a day off. But it was unavoidable.

I set my alarm to seven thirty, and was in Andres's chair by nine. I was tired as hell, but it'd be packed if I waited. Better now than never.

Knock-knock.

My text notification went off as I scrolled through my phone apps to access the drop screen.

Teddy: *Wyd ;p*

Me: *Getting a haircut*

I held my phone out for a few, even though I wasn't expecting an immediate reply or one at all. Sometimes that was how Teddy got in your head. Best case scenario, she just wanted to see how long it'd take for a reply. By the time I lowered my phone to my lap—

Knock-knock.

Teddy: *Oooohhhh, lemme see*

Me: *Not done yet*

Teddy: *Working?*

Me: *Day off*

Direct responses were best. I didn't want to bring up that bad trip weeks back, figuring the second I brought it up, she'd never want to speak to me again. Two ignored texts and three phone calls only confirmed it. Yet here we were.

Teddy: *That's what's up XD*

Me: *What are you up to?*

Teddy: *Not much*

Me: *Read anything cool?*

Teddy: *Yeah XD*

I knew that was what she liked. Outside of Spike and Singleton movies, music in Spanish, and messing with your mind.

Teddy: *You're so cute*

Definitely trying to mind-fuck me.

Me: *Stop trying to make me smile*

Teddy: *Is it working?*

Me: *Yes :)*

Teddy: *I want to see you*

I brought the camera lens of my phone to face level. The cut was fresh but wasn't styled in the way I usually wore it, but I still asked Andres to step out from the shot. Snapping a few selfies, I sent them over.

Teddy: *I want to see you for real now*

Me: *Picture not enough?*

Teddy: *Unless you have plans*

It wouldn't be much longer. Should I bite?

Me: *Can be there in less than an hour*

Teddy: *K*

I didn't overthink things. If Teddy wanted to get up, I knew what the expectation was. The situation was complicated, but at least the sex wasn't. She did what she wanted and didn't care what people thought about it. For that reason, we clicked.

Teddy wasn't always the easiest friend to have, but most times the benefits outweighed the risks. Reggie was never even an afterthought. They were never serious to begin with, so by now I'd stopped feeling bad about it. All I cared about was how Teddy made me feel. Until that changed, this was how we were with each other.

* * *

"You rode your skateboard here? You should've told me. I would've picked you up."

I followed Teddy past the broken elevator to the stairwell. Letting her lead the way gave me the best view of her ass in that tight-ass pink dress, and it was making me horny thinking of our history with stairwells. I took two extra steps to hook my arm around her as she reached over to bury her fingers in my hair.

My lips invaded, raiding her neck, expelling giggles and gentle slaps against my arm. "You're so stupid Asher," left her mouth, but I knew she liked it. She turned to claim my lips with her own, tongues thrusting back and forth. My hand dropped the skateboard (even though it's an FTC), so Teddy got the full ten digits exploring that lovely figure of hers. I reached under her dress, eliciting a scream I didn't expect.

"Mmm…not here," she said with a smile.

I bit my lip, then drew in to kiss her. "You know how *well* we do in stairwells…"

Eventually Teddy convinced me how nosy the neighbors around here were and that only two floors separated us from having some *real* fun. But two floors felt like forever when you wanted it bad.

"Your hair looks better in person," she continued, waiting for me at the door marked with "4."

She reached for my locks again, but I had to lean over so she could touch them without having to strain. "I swear I hate how tall you are. It's annoying."

"It's not my fault you're so friggin' tiny," I said with a laugh.

"Yeah, tiny. *Sure.*" Teddy was thick, but that didn't change the ten inches between us.

Once we were near her apartment door, I picked her up, eliciting another high-pitched outcry. She hid her face behind her hand in a fit of titters.

"All this giggling."

"I'm just giggling because I'm surprised you can carry my fat ass."

Wow. We had extremely different definitions of how her body looked. "Girls are fucking weird."

"It's not like I don't think I look good, but I got like, fifteen pounds on you. What are you—like, one-fifty? One-sixty?"

"One-ninety. On a good day." My body was muscular, but I was on the lean side. My height made up for most of it, but a hundred sixty pounds? I was offended. I wasn't one of those dudes who were only built for small frames. I could handle them all. She shied away from me as she opened her front door, but took my hand on the short glide from her kitchen to her room.

She leaned into kiss me once we were inches from her bed. I spread out on top of her the moment her back connected to the mattress. Her hands caressed the small of my back, exploring my skin the higher they traveled. The warmth of her hands brought tinges of heat with each touch. She pulled my shirt over my head, as I flipped her over onto my lap.

Don't think, just do. I kept repeating that in my head until I followed through to the end. Teddy grinding her body against my body made it easier. I let my hands do the thinking, as they felt the softness of the back of Teddy's thighs. Her body jumped when I gave that gorgeous ass of hers a good smack. She kissed my neck, making me a slave to her mercy.

"Shit." My voice cracked in a laugh. If only girls knew how much we liked that. She didn't stop there. Her sexy, full lips etched breathtaking sensations along every inch worthy of their attention. She spent extra attention on my chest, trying to break *me* down before things even went down. By now, she'd crawled off the side of her bed, and she rested on her knees to the floor, playing with my zipper.

She gently rubbed my cock through the fabric of my jeans, waking my body up for more action. With a swipe of her hand, my zipper came down, and she pulled me out of my boxers and traced a long line with her tongue from my balls to the head of my shaft.

"Go easy, Teddy. I'm, like, not going to be able to last if you go full throttle."

Teddy laughed me off, helping me pull out of my jeans. A combination of short feathery licks with wet pillowy lips massaged my length, tensing up my upper body.

"You are so fucking good at this, Teddy."

She took half of me in her mouth, splashing and circling her tongue against my shaft, teasing me with each surprise technique her mouth had in store. I pulled her hair from her face, balling fistfuls of it in my hand. Teddy reached one of her hands to caress my stomach and chest. "Okay, that's good."

Just to tease, she took all of me in her mouth one last time. I needed to remember to return the favor when it was her turn to squirm. I pulled a condom from my pocket and slid it on with just enough space left at the tip.

I took Teddy's hand and helped her on the bed, pulling her dress over her head. Mmm… Just the sight of her dark brown skin in her light blue underwear made me bite my lip. I admired the soft feel of her body and the visual of healthy legs, tummy, and breasts. Nothing was flat on her, but I didn't want it to be. I crawled over her, pinning her to one spot.

"Do you want me to fuck you?" Teddy nibbled her lower lip and nodded. I adjusted her body toward the middle of the bed and teased her knees open.

I could already tell how turned on she was, but I was in a eating-out mood. Hovering over her pelvis, I pushed her panties to the side and feasted. Using my tongue to free her delicious clit from her *other* lips, I licked her just to remember what she tasted like. It surprised me when she pushed my head away. Hard.

"Damn, girl, you must ready," I said as I dragged her body closer to mine.

I spit on my hand and rubbed it on the condom for lube. Resting one of her ankles on my shoulder, I slowly thrust into her, met with a slight resistance. I swore, working my way up to a gradual rhythm. I held Teddy's thigh, using it for balance, watching my body thrust deeper into hers. I slowed down the pace when I noticed Teddy's face in a pained grimace, until it made me stop altogether.

"Am I hurting you?"

Teddy opened her eyes, the grip her inner thighs had on my waist tightening. "Only when you're all the way inside me," she snapped back.

"It's because I didn't go down on you." Come to think of it, Teddy always got that tongue action before I did anything else to her. I only hadn't this time because she'd pushed me away. I pulled out of her.

"Get on your knees."

"I don't want you to go down on me now."

Said by no girl ever. "Why?"

"I haven't waxed in like, three weeks."

I slipped over to the foot of the bed until I was on the floor. "Teddy, just get on your knees."

She bent over toward the foot of the bed, awarding me the opportunity to kiss the back of her thighs, her cheeks, the outside of her panties. I pulled her panties to one side and buried my tongue between her lips. A slight tremble shook her body against mine and only intensified when I flicked my tongue against her clit.

She edged up slightly to watch my mouth bury itself between her legs, teasing her with fast, yet soft motions as I positioned myself underneath her. She turned her attention to the floor and smiled when she turned back to me.

"Are you touching yourself?" she giggled.

Eating pussy made me horny as hell. It was hard not experiencing my own fun during the process. Teddy crawled off my face, inviting me back to bed with her. It was high time to pull her out of those panties for good this time. She took the initiative and pushed me down to the bed to climb on top of me. A flush of relief dressed her features as she lowered her body onto mine with ease. I pushed her bra down, exposing her sweet tits to me to suck and play with while she brought herself up and down on my dick.

"Mmm… Don't worry about me, Teddy. Just fuck me the way you like it." My mouth stayed busy sucking and nibbling the fullness of each nipple in front of me. The resistance was now gone as her body stretched to accommodate me. I grabbed her hips and took turns pumping into her, to match the rise and fall of her devouring my whole cock.

"You feel so good, Asher," she moaned, digging her nails into my shoulder.

"You like that?"

But she didn't have to answer. The grimace she wore now wasn't from pain this time, only pleasure. And by the looks of it, she was close. Dirty swears and breathy moans championed me to keep at it. Her upper body convulsed as she gave out and collapsed on top of me. Her lips dragged all over my neck and shoulders.

I was ready to lose myself inside her. I wrapped my arms around her body to steady her from falling as I flipped her on her back. My body was ready for that numbing release it so badly craved. Spreading her creamy thighs apart, I drove my frenzied pelvis back and forth to meet her hips, hard and desperate to reach a breaking point. The minute she opened her mouth with all that Spanish shit, electric sensations fired up, intensifying the spasms in my groin.

I grabbed hold of her thighs, drawing the tension someplace else, and two, long strokes were all I needed to pass out next to her. A mix of salt, sweat, and the flavor of each other blended together as our lips devoured each other with want and need. Teddy pulled off the condom and threw it away as I reached for my boxers on the floor.

Teddy hopped back on the bed, working her fingers through my hair again. I was already drowsy—she was about to make matters worse.

"Seriously, Teddy, if you're not trying to make me fall asleep, I wouldn't do that." It was like she knew the right place to touch to soothe, provoke, or arouse me. But playing with my hair, on top of just having sex, after I'd gotten up early this morning, was a deadly combination to put me to sleep.

* * *

Teddy

I didn't think he'd actually fall asleep. Was it that serious? I didn't mind, though. He looked so cute in his sleep. Six feet, two inches of tattooed tough guy, thwarted by having his hair played with.

I didn't want to wake him, but I was bored. My appetite for something sweet was uncontrollable at this point. A round-trip ticket from my room to the kitchen was a necessary destination. I planned on going to town on those leftover guava and cheese empanadas from Mami Rita's. Even at room temperature, they were so damn good.

Knock-knock.

My phone alerted on the coffee table. At least, I think it was my phone. I positioned Asher's skateboard under the table and picked up the phone to unlock the screen.

Derek: *Thinking about you makes my dick so hard right now...*

Whoa. Not my phone. They were the exact model, so I didn't notice until I picked it up. A dozen thoughts rushed to my head. It wasn't my business, but I didn't know that much about Asher aside from a few interests. I was surprised he'd even come over, recalling our last encounter. He was one of my friends. Maybe one of my better ones. But I wasn't sure he wanted me to know that.

I raced back to my room, with my own phone this time, preoccupying my boredom with seventeen minutes of *Candy Crush* before Asher showed any signs of life. I was hungry for real food and couldn't wait for him to wake up.

"Shit. What time is it?" Asher said, rubbing his face.

"A little past three. I was about to go out, so…"

Asher nodded, reaching for his shirt and pants on the other side of the bed. I watched him slip his athletic build back into his clothes, a body that was a mix of natural muscle and maybe a little added effort. For what it was worth, it flattered his height without being bulky.

"You can come with me if you're not doing anything." I left it open-ended.

Asher hesitated. "I'm not trying to cramp your style if you're meeting up with somebody."

I shook my head. "I'm not meeting up with anyone. Just thought I'd take a ride. Wasn't sure if I wanted to go alone. You're here. I'm asking you."

Asher didn't look thrilled with the idea. To take the pressure off, I receded the invitation.

"It's cool if you don't want to. If you got what you came for, it's not a big deal."

By the time I was halfway to my door, Asher finally answered back.

"I'll take a ride."

* * *

Psychedelic Spanish pop filled the confines of my car. I loved how it had a Nuevo disco vibe. It reminded me of Marina & The Diamonds, but way better because it was in Spanish. When I sang to the lyrics, I lost myself in the syncopated electric bass, so in the zone I forgot Ash was sitting shotgun.

I was met with a wide smile and glowing eyes.

"See, now you messed with my vibe." I couldn't possibly keep singing now that I knew I had an audience.

"No, you're good," he said, running his tongue across his teeth. I hit him, and he play-pretended it hurt like hell. He was so corny.

"I'm just looking out for those high notes." He mocked the sounds I made when we had sex. Asshole.

I turned my eyes from the wheel for a second to mock him back. "Don't confuse the way you have Derek, with me." It came out so fast, I didn't realize I'd said it until it was too late.

"What are you looking through my phone or something?" Asher asked defensively.

I tried to play it off as a joke, but wasn't very successful. "Thought it was my phone. My bad."

There was a long pause, the conversation dropping from one hundred to zero. I had to say something. "Do you mess with him?"

Asher sighed, like he was either bored or downright annoyed.

He must've been used to being asked. "Are you asking me because you actually want to know? Or are you asking to see if I'll lie?"

"Just asking a question." Now he was going to think I was a stalker, checking for his messages. While the conversation was fresh, I was still curious. I wasn't marching in any pride parades anytime soon, but I wasn't just straight.

"Sometimes."

That was something I didn't hear every day. I wondered if my silence scared him into thinking I didn't approve.

"I hook up with this girl sometimes. She has a boyfriend, but not when we're chilling. You know how it is." I said to no one in particular.

"That's good to know." Not the best way to show camaraderie, but the rest of the way to South Beach was painfully quiet. It was a relief to be around people again, even though the parking lot was packed to the rim. Asher was busy on his phone and didn't seem in the best mood for talking.

Maybe I shouldn't have asked him to come. Or maybe I shouldn't have brought up the phone thing. But either way, it looked like the rest of the day would be a drag.

"I'm about to look for a place to eat. Not sure if you're down." I said, waiting for him to turn me away or get out the car.

When he didn't answer me back, I turned on my heel and headed for the boardwalk. I stopped to better assess which restaurants would suit my appetite best. A figure bumped into me, steadying their hand against my shoulder. Ash. I faked a smile, and we stalked in silence across the congested boardwalk. Avid rollerbladers darted past, leaving remains of their dust in our direction. I didn't feel much like sharing, but I didn't know what else to say to change the mood.

"I have Hodgkin's lymphoma." It felt like I'd been holding it in, with never a real chance to say it. We were friends, but I'd never told anyone that didn't need to know. But it was either go on saying nothing or that.

Asher's face was scrunched in confusion when I actually had the courage to face him. "Isn't that, like, cancer?"

"I'm not repeating myself." I wiped away at the tears to force them not to come down.

Asher rubbed the side of his face before reaching in his wallet to fetch a cigarette. He lit it, then took a drag and held it out for me to take. "That sucks."

I went for the hit, smooth and bold. It wasn't like weed, but it calmed the nerves either way. "I know."

* * *

In our search, we found a Peruvian mom-and-pop that satisfied both our cravings. We sat in a booth nursing two coconuts waters, but the most of what we said was to the wait staff. I wasn't even sure we were going to talk until he broke the silence.

"Can I ask about it?"

The waiter brought out his lomo saltado, with my aji de gallina. He set each plate down and asked if we needed anything more. We were all set for now, but if we needed them, we'd let them know.

"Only if I can ask about you," I said with a full mouth. The velvety stew awakened my taste buds. I needed a Peruvian friend yesterday to serve this up all the time.

"Deal. You can ask about me if I can ask about you."

"Can I go first?" Asher nodded as I wrestled with a napkin. "Are you bi? Because you know you can tell me. I don't care."

Asher clucked his tongue and shot me a blank look. "I don't do labels."

"Well, are you attracted more to girls or guys?"

He broke out in a short laughter. "I fucking hate that question."

"Why?"

"Teddy, I am, like, so fucking attracted to you it's not even funny. But as soon as a person hears I like dudes, what *they* hear is that I must automatically not like girls. Or that I'm really just gay, but confused. There isn't a percentage level to how much I'm into a person. And being attracted to men doesn't make me any less attracted to a woman. And I'm not thinking about anything but you when I'm with you. Especially how incredibly hot you look when I'm fucking the shit out of you."

It wasn't the sweetest thing to say. But it was one hundred percent Asher. That made me like hearing it more.

"Is it my turn now?"

I was nervous, nodding reluctantly as I hid behind my coconut water.

"Is it bad?"

"Define bad."

"Chemo? Hospital trips—"

"Then it's bad. And aggressive."

The color drained from Asher's face, a grimace emerging as he shook his head in disbelief. "How long have you had it?"

"Since I was a teenager. Off and on. It'll go into remission, but so far it's always come back." It wasn't worth faking a smile for.

"I would've never guessed that. You look so healthy."

I went on to explain how I'd managed to gain fifty pounds when at times it was hard to gain any. Vanity was my vice.

"Is that why you smoke so much weed?" he asked, trying to lighten the mood. It worked, but not by much.

"Yes and no." To say I only smoked weed during chemo was a lie. I would've loved it regardless of my Hodgkin's.

"Does it scare you?"

I faked a smirk, but I doubt it looked convincing. "I guess."

Asher tousled his food on his fork and reached out to squeeze my hand. "I'm not trying to upset you. It's just…you said I could ask."

It didn't help much, but at least I had someone new to talk to about it.

We ended up exploring most of East Side, but aside from not wanting to get my hair wet, we didn't have anything to swim in, so we mainly browsed the shops. I don't know why either of us didn't just call it a night, but we ran with it and made a day of it. By the time we got back to my place, we even gave *Clockers* a rewatch. I think we were too baked and horny to remember where we'd left off last time, and since it played all the way to the end, we watched back from the beginning.

Somewhere between Strike's brother being brought in by the cop and Rodney's enforcer getting shot, things got a little hands-on. Asher wasn't shy about ignoring the movie. Kissing turned into rubbing. Rubbing turned into touching. Before I knew it, Asher's face was lodged between my legs again. I loved how he made me forget. Even when I was pissed off at everything, I needed to forget sometimes.

"I'm starting to think *Clockers* is too much of an aphrodisiac for us," I moaned, thighs twitching against Asher's face. "Asher, stop."

He brought his body up toward me and wiped off his mouth and chin. He studied me with curious eyes, waiting for the reason for the holdup.

"I like you. Reggie's my friend. I'm not trying to play you. That's just…how it is."

Asher's mouth thinned into a straight line, like he was ready to reconsider. He took a deep breath and nodded. "Okay."

CHAPTER TEN

Teddy

I didn't know how I'd survive without marijuana. Some people demonized it, and why not? It was easier to. But there were too many times I didn't know how I'd cope without it. Some days I was okay, most days I was fine.

But those days never made up for the days I wasn't fine. Sometimes it took more energy than I had to get out of bed. Bringing myself to shower, get dressed, or drive? Even when my body refused to eat, at least I had a little appetite after a smoke. It curbed the pain too...*sometimes*.

Smoking always seemed like the one thing that gave me control over my body.

My body.

At times my best friend, others my worst enemy. Shouldn't I be used to it? You never get used to the way your body betrays you.

My fingers reached for my bedside dresser in the dark. I should've kept my medical alert on, but I was embarrassed to wear it. I wanted to avoid: *"What is that for?"* and *"You don't look sick..."* and *"Why do you need that?"*

My body washed itself in sweat, the heat from the fever making my eyelids too hot or heavy to open, making it difficult to press that little red button. The one that would save me if I were in too much pain to save myself.

"Theodora King, we're following up a distress call. Do you require assistance?"

I rolled over to my side. I hid the receiver under the bed, but it picked up my voice well so all I had to do was speak loud and clear.

"Yeah, I'm not doing so hot." My voice was pained but broke as if I were laughing.

"Your address is 2000 North Bayshore Drrive, Miami, Flordia, zip code 33137?"

"Yes."

"We're sending someone over. Stay with me."

Counting the minutes it took for an ambulance to get here, the operator spent that time asking me about my symptoms and to rate the pain on a scale from one to ten. It was for sure a nine, but instead I told her eight since it wasn't the worse I'd experienced. Most likely, she was only asking as suffer porn.

When the ambulance arrived, it all happened at a speed I couldn't register. I was wheeled into the back of a medical truck. They attached an IV to my arm and explained it was for the pain, but it made me blink in and out. I didn't even know where I was after a few minutes with this thing.

Sometimes my imagination took me all these different places as I dazed in and out of consciousness, usually to worlds in books I'd read and reread. The one bit that constantly replayed itself was a scene right out of an Octavia Butler book, where the main character Lilith opens her eyes faced with Jdatya for the first time, scared out of her wits.

Octavia Butler's *Xenogenesis* series gave me nightmares, but it never stopped me from devouring them over and over again. Maybe I saw myself in Lilith, a dark-skinned black girl in a world I didn't always understand, envisioning being disgusted by tentacles, every time they tensed violently against its alien body until he was willing to close its skin to appear grey and smooth.

It was a crazy dream, but I always woke up at the best part. Jdatya admitting he'd experimented on me, testing and removing a tumor from my body—only instead of a tumor, it was my Hodgkin's. Like Lilith, I felt so violated, but the thought was lost after finding out I was free of cancer. It was always so real. I always woke up wondering why it was never that easy.

It was the middle of the next day by the time I had the energy to open my eyes again but not much energy for anything else. A small white hospital room, the only place in my life I'd ever seen more than my own apartment. Having Hodgkin's, sterile white rooms were a part of me, a part of my identity as much as being *Cubana*, as much as being Black.

I had nightmares with hideous aliens, had nights worse than that one, had been told countless times I didn't respond well to most treatments, but none of them put fear in me quite like the sight of a little white room.

* * *

Was it me or the opioids? My medicine cabinet at home certainly rivaled Betty Ford's, but I preferred weed, only using the prescriptions when it was necessary. But when you're in a room complaining about pain, they give you whatever they think will shut you up. I was fighting and losing myself in and out of consciousness.

I was bored, lonely, tired, and disoriented, but none of that stopped me from picking up the room phone. I dialed what came to memory. I was good at memorizing numbers, but not so good at remembering who they belonged to. My mami never picked up the phone. Maybe that's where I got it from. But it didn't stop me from leaving a groggy message on her voicemail not remembering half of what I'd said. She knew me well enough to know when I took something, so the least I'd get would be a call back later in the day. Hell, I didn't even know what time it was.

The second number I dialed picked up on the third ring. Or was it fourth? I wasn't keeping track, my brain wouldn't let me.

"Hello?" the person on the other end said. Reggie.

"Hey, Reggie," I said, slurring my words.

"Who's this?"

"You know who this is." I rubbed my face, trying to rub the tired off me, but it wasn't working.

"Girl, are you high?"

I shrugged, even though he couldn't see that through the phone. "No. So what if I am? That's the only time you ever want to see me. When I have weed." I was high, but it was true. Even when I was sober I thought that. He'd never given me a reason to think otherwise, aside from asking if I'd be his girl or not. I liked being around him. I wouldn't still have his number memorized if I didn't. But his motivation behind wanting something serious only seemed genuine after I started messing around with Ash. It was like he could sense someone else wanted me just as much as him. Sometimes it seemed liked he only wanted me more when he knew someone else did.

"Teddy, I can't talk to you like this. Call me back when you're lucid."

"Don't hang up on me!" I said a second too late. I can't believe that fool hung up on me. I needed to talk to someone. All I was asking was for someone to hear me. Too drowsy to be anything more than pissed, I dialed the number back, hoping for a response.

It wasn't until the fifth ring someone picked up, and when the voice on the other end spoke, I realized I'd gotten the numbers mixed up. "Hello?"

I hesitated before asking "Hello?" back, like a dumb ass.

The voice on the other end followed up with an uncertain tone. "Who's this?"

I tried to articulate my name, but it was the only word I couldn't say right now. "I must know you because I know you're number…"

"Teddy? You okay?"

"No… Yes… I don't know." I adjusted my pillow underneath my head, but with an IV in my arm, nothing I did made it more comfortable. "There's a lot of medicine in me." I did my best to sound coherent, but morphine and me didn't go together. "I don't know what I'm doing."

"Where are you?" Asher asked with a level of certainty this time.

"A lymphoma center in North Miami." That yawn in between came out of nowhere. "I'm just bored. Lonely. High, I guess. What are you doing?"

I dozed on and off, listening to Ash explain that he was at work and what he did in that cash office when he wasn't on the floor. I'd wake up every once in a while to hear my name being repeated through the receiver a few times, asking me to stay with him, even though he knew I was drowsy.

I couldn't help it, though. My eyes eventually closed, falling victim to the effects of the drugs.

* * *

I didn't check the time before I dozed off, but my guess was that it couldn't have been long. I was nowhere near refreshed. When I came to, someone was sitting across from me, resting their face in their hand.

At the sight of my movement, they readjusted themselves in the chair, peering their piercing eyes at me. I covered my face with the unfitted sheet on the bed, which did little to muffle the rasp of his laugh. "Oh my god…How did you know I was here?"

"Because you told me, dummy."

My subconscious knew enough about earlier to remember I'd spoken to Ash, but what we'd talked about had never traveled to the rest of my brain.

"Why did you come?"

"You said I could." Lie. By the time I took the sheet from my eyes, the smile on his face and eyes revealed it to be his own truth. "I wanted to see if you were doing okay. It was hard to tell over the phone. I would've left once I saw you were fine, but when I went to rub your shoulder, you grabbed my hand. I thought you were awake, so I waited."

We all had our own lives, so my support group didn't visit each other in hospitals as much. Or at least not like chemo checkups. We did when it was Racer, but we all knew why we made time for him. Outside of them, I didn't have any other friends who would come check up on me just to see if I were okay. In their defense, they didn't know. But I never wanted them to. I'm not sure I wanted other people to see me in such a vulnerable state. To most girls, vulnerability was letting someone see them without makeup. With me? Let's just say, it was hard to pretend nothing was wrong when you had an IV in your arm, going in and out of consciousness due to painkillers. This wasn't a comfortable situation for me. I couldn't imagine it being any more comfortable to witness.

Whatever Asher was thinking, he hid it well. Any discomfort he felt was disguised behind that baby-faced grin of his. A part of me didn't want his comfort. I didn't want this to be as normal to him as it was for me.

"How long have you been here?" I asked, shifting underneath the sheet, extending my legs.

Asher curled his lips, considering. "Twenty minutes maybe?"

"Oh." I blinked twice, and when I opened my eyes again, Asher was just a few inches from my face.

"You seem totally out of it Teddy."

"It's because of whatever they're pumping me with." I covered my face with all my fingers, massaging my eyelids with my palms. "I wish Reggie was here." I kept remembering he was who I'd meant to call. I was glad to see Asher, but I was too beyond spaced out to know what I was saying. My mind was everywhere right now, including Reggie. I couldn't remember whether I was mad or happy.

"Well…I guess I'll let go… Let you get some sleep." His lips pressed tight together in a thin line, and I was sure he didn't see me when I waved a slow, heavy wave on his way to the door. Once he was halfway out, he turned and shot me a salute sign from across the room and disappeared into the hallway.

I fought hard against sleep, but I lost.

* * *

These nurses had to be sick and tired of me. Now that I'd come to, I was more myself. There was still some pain, but nothing worth staying for. My symptoms just got the best of me. Most days I could handle it. I was scheduled for chemotherapy in the next two weeks, so I wasn't about to spend two more days here. Right now I just wanted to be home.

The cab ride left me plenty of time to think. I'd called Reggie while I was at the center. Asshole hung up on me. Seriously, later for him. Dude better not call or text me when he wanted something or someone to talk to. This was why I kept him right where he was supposed to be. Yeah, we were friends. But if you couldn't handle a sixty-second phone call with me strung out, what made you think you could handle a fucking relationship?

I couldn't remember why I'd even wanted one. I'd never been more miserable than in one. Waiting on someone's calls or texts.

Worrying about stupid people in their phone. Being ignored. I could get all those things single, and at least I wouldn't have someone calling me crazy.

Sometimes the only person I felt had my back was Asher.

Asher was cool. He was better than cool. But people change with titles. He said so himself—he didn't do titles. If I would've had a say, I wouldn't have seen him at all, but it was nice of him to visit. I couldn't even remember what we'd talked about, but his presence was nice.

My phone was out of the charger when I got home, but there was still enough battery to check my messages. Hmph. None from Asher. I went ahead and texted him.

Me: *Fell asleep on you...*

I was hoping to see him while I wasn't on morphine. Especially since my chemo would leave me drained the first week and I'd have next to no drive to do anything the week after. When I didn't hear back from him, I checked my other messages.

One was from Monica, but it was only to say she got back with her boyfriend. Guess I could cancel her out for a while. I got a few threads going on from my support group buddies, but I'd probably pass on the next session. I wasn't up to it like last time. I wasn't going to even acknowledge the messages from a few strangers I was hoping would just stop. Everything.

But the two from Reggie stood out on their own. *"What's good with you?"* and *"You all right?"* Like he cared. They were time-stamped five hours ago.

Me: *Some ole.*

Which he'd know, if I could actually trust him. I didn't want fake pity or pretend concern. I knew he cared about me. Sometimes. But he didn't have a good way of showing it when I seemed healthy, and I wasn't about to deal with it sick. I was glad the first person I ever told who wasn't dealing with something similar was Asher. He didn't make me feel like he could make it all better or that shit was going to get better with hope.

The only things he'd ever ask were how things went, referring to the chemotherapy, and if I wanted to talk about it. If I didn't, he dropped it. If I did, we talked. But it was never on some *"Everything is going to be fine with hope"* crap. Trust me, most of my cancer buddies *hate* hearing that from abled folk.

My phone vibrated with life, and I investigated the screen. Rats. Just Reggie.

Reggie: *You trying to get up?*

Me: *To do what?*

Reggie: *What you mean what?*

Me: *Just sayin', seem like you're always busy. Don't you 'not' have time?*

Reggie: *So why you call me then?*

Me: *To talk. You hung up. Moving on.*

Reggie: *Couldn't understand you. Could call me now :o*

Me: *Rather not. Ain't trying to take up your precious time.*

A few texts flooded my phone, followed by a phone call. It was like he was trying to get on my nerves. When my phone died, I was relieved. I went to the kitchen to make a mix between a smoothie and a shake. I was hungry but wasn't down for heavy food. I turned on the TV and tuned into a streaming app. If I was going to be bored, might as well be entertained.

CHAPTER ELEVEN

Asher

I didn't check my phone until I was off. I tossed it in my locker. Didn't seem like I'd be needing it on the clock. I was stressed out enough.

I feel asleep on you...

That among other things. I deleted the message, clocked out, and met up with Reggie at the exit. I wasn't looking forward to the bus.

If there was one thing I hated more than Miami's humidity, it was its transit system. It was neither cheap, nor convenient. I couldn't even remember the last time I filled my Easy Card as my bike was my main source of transportation. It sucked that I didn't know shit about motorcycle repair. Since I needed my brakes done, I was without a ride for a few days.

It only took a week to get sick of the way the bus system worked. Want to get to work on time? Leave an hour and a half early. Most bus drivers were overworked and underpaid, so they didn't give a shit if being late threw off your schedule. It could be worse, though. Like being unemployed. Sometimes if Reggie got off the same time and he had his grandmother's whip, he'd spot me a ride. If not, we'd chill until one of our buses came.

I wasn't a fan of nights like this, when I was the closing manager. Busy nights like tonight guaranteed not getting off before ten, the time I needed a cigarette most. Reggie got off a half-hour before, but the bus to take us both to Northside Station didn't leave until a few minutes after I clocked out.

We'd part ways from there, but the wait for the #2 to downtown Miami couldn't end soon enough.

"I'm mad they cut my hours to two days next week," Reggie said, preoccupied by something on his phone.

If only I had the luxury. Sometimes I was so sick of that place, I wished I could call out every shift. "Dude, I can't relate. I'm getting worked up until next week. I'm looking forward to those two consecutive days off I got coming to me. I better not hear no phone calls."

I inhaled, blowing smoke out my mouth and nose. Reggie's produce position awarded him the freedom to go on break whenever he wanted and stretch out two hours of work for an entire shift, so I wasn't feeling sorry anytime soon. But I was sympathetic. He did have bills to pay.

Reggie flicked his nearly smoked cigarette to the ground. He mentioned a few work-related things, then changed the subject. "Let me tell you what happened the other day with Teddy—"

Here we go again. Reggie was my boy, but he talked too much most the time. About everything. Work. Home. Girls. Sometimes I just wanted to feel the high of the nicotine and bounce. It was cool when we were high, but he brought up Teddy every once in a while and it wasn't always easy keeping my face straight.

The things he complained about when it came to Teddy were things I would never know. I saw Teddy—her real side, her vulnerable side—so it was hard to hear him talk shit. I'll admit I wasn't the expert on all things Teddy, but come one—you'd have to be blind to not see she was a little depressed. So she didn't answer a few phone calls now and then. If I was dealing with what she was dealing with, I'm sure a few phone calls would slip my mind, too. Maybe he'd known her longer, but I knew her better. I braced myself for whatever he was about to tell me. It was about to be a long wait for the bus.

"I can't stand to say this, but you know I'm feeling her mad hard right?"

I scratched the side of my face, rubbing the five o'clock shadow I was working with. "I'm sure you've mentioned that several times." I tried my best not to sound sarcastic but failed miserably. "Matter fact, you never stop mentioning that every time she comes up in conversation."

"This is how I know you've never been fucked up by someone."

I wanted to laugh so bad, but at the risk of blowing my spot, I leaned away on the bench, hands up, palms facing Reggie. "Dude, I'm just making an observation."

This was the third or fourth time since I'd met Teddy that he'd mentioned his issue about their relationship. If I was forced to listen to it once again, I would at least voice my frustration. Regardless of how I put myself in the situation.

"Reggie, when I met her, what was one of the first things you said to me about her?"

"When you first met her? Motherfucker, I don't know!" Reggie flinched his head back, an edge to his forced laughter.

"Well, since you don't remember, I'm about to remind you. *Teddy's cool. We have fun. But she's not girlfriend material.* That's what you said. I'm not trying to come at you sideways bro, but one minute you say she is, the next minute she isn't. Which one is it? Because if I was dealing with you, I'd be on some bullshit, too."

Reggie liked to talk, but only when you were telling him what he wanted to hear. He shifted and squirmed on the bench and kicked the air like a little-ass kid. "You just hear one side of the story and make up your mind that I'm the petty one. But you don't see the shit she puts me through. The mind-fucks she gives me—"

"Does Teddy exhibit any new behavior? Is this dance really all that new to you?"

"No, but seriously. Wouldn't you be mad if you put yourself out there and a chick just stomped all over you, like you weren't shit?"

I knew where Reg was going with this, and he wasn't alone in feeling some kind of way when it came to Teddy. Sometimes I hated her, how she treated me, how I let her treat me, and how I let myself get treated. I wanted her so bad. All to myself. But everything was a choice. There was no gun to my head. No knife at my side. No rope around my throat. Every moment with her, I knew deep down she was probably playing me. But I didn't care.

"Let me break it down how this looks to me," I continued, picking off finger by finger all the examples of how things from the outside appeared. "She's not up your ass, which when she was you took issue with. She's probably the finest girl I've ever seen you bag, no offense. She's fucking honest with you instead of telling you things you want to hear. *None* of the shit you're feeling should be a surprise to you. In fact, I wish I was fucking you right now."

"You're just saying that because you don't have to deal with it." If only he knew how wrong he was. "I put myself out there, and now she want to act like I'm the one who brought the idea up in the first place."

I leaned my elbow on my knee, nursing the vein protruding near my forehead. "I only know what you tell me. I don't know the middle shit. But I have a feeling no matter what I say, you're going to ignore my advice anyway. I can't help you, so I'm not interested in hearing all your dirty laundry, so this better be the last time I hear about this shit."

Reggie wanted things to be serious between them, but I knew

she liked my attention too much to end things. I had a lot to think about, wanting to be a better friend, but resentment made me a bitter one. When the #2 bus came into view, I shot Reggie a salute and prepared myself for the hardest decision I might have to make right now.

CHAPTER TWELVE

Asher

I'd thought a lot about my last conversation with Reggie, never considering the consequence of how it'd affect our friendship if he ever got wise to what Teddy and I did on the side. The whole thing just rubbed me the wrong way. I knew Teddy had feelings for him. Or, at least, had at one point. From the last time we talked, he was feeling her hard. I couldn't help but feel like my presence was a huge inconvenience. That I complicated things. Teddy wasn't the type of girl who had you around when she wasn't interested. Maybe I was selfish for wanting her, but if she and Reggie had a thing some time ago, then maybe what we had right now was a thing, too. Sure, Reggie had feelings for her, but did that mean I wasn't allowed to?

Was I a better friend than boyfriend material? I think I made her happy. But I was lucky if I saw her twice, maybe three times in one month. How often did he see her? How many times had I been her second choice after he hadn't come through? These were the things I asked myself because I didn't know the answers off-hand. How much would it hurt to take myself out of the equation? Personally, I didn't know how much I could take of this back-and-forth shit, and I honestly knew that backing out now could save our friendship—both mine and his and hers and mine.

We'd planned to chill on Sunday, my one day off this week. She asked if I wanted to do something or stay in, and I had no objection to either one. Teddy was my only friend who I was one hundred percent honest with all the time. To say we only chilled to have sex was…just not the truth. She picked me up when I needed her. We went out and had fun. Once we even drove six hours flea market hopping to replace some high-priced headphones she'd dropped in the sink while we were…*busy* with other things.

She was my homie, my lover, my friend. Now that I knew her, it was hard to imagine life without her. But I'd always been the middleman. A thorn in the side of what Reggie and Teddy could possibly have. I couldn't be Teddy's friend, not with the relationship that we had, and be Reggie's go-to guy when it came to her. It sucked. Really sucked. But I put myself in the position to catch feelings—who else could I blame but myself? Things were going to get ugly. I knew they would. So I contemplated ways on how to fix it, end it. Before it reached a point of no return.

We ate at some fusion Brazilian-Japanese joint, and afterward, out of boredom, we decided to blaze up. That I hoped wouldn't change. The sex would be hard to walk away from, but a session buddy? I didn't want to lose everything that made our friendship great. I brought over a different strain, and Teddy was good at smoking me out. I always felt tired and composed and sometimes I preferred that sativa feel, but the only downside with kush was that it made her crazy horny.

When you were high, you were aware, but you didn't think things through as much. That conversation I'd planned on having? It would have to wait. We were too deep in a make out session to quit right that second. I told myself I'd stopped if she kissed me. Then I convinced myself I'd stop if she groped me.

When she reached for my zipper, a trickle of common sense flooded into me, forcing me to deal with the subject I'd waited too long to address.

"Mmm…Teddy." I said, pushing her away from me. "Teddy, stop." Which came out breathless and hard to take seriously.

"Why? I just want to taste you," she said seductively, proceeding to unzip my zipper with her teeth. I wanted her to taste me. Shit, I almost let her. But in the split second it took watching her, I remembered why I'd planned to talk to her in the first place. I needed to put an end to our benefits package, and it took all the strength in the world to playfully get her to stop. She didn't.

"No, seriously. Come on." My voice shook, as if I almost didn't mean it. Like she was waiting for me to yell sike and let things continue on. PSA: I wanted them to.

"I think we need to chill out, you know?"

She ignored my words, with that *"I want to fuck you"* look in her eyes as she kissed on my stomach. I had to stay focused.

"You're making this shit so much harder." I leaned up and pulled down on my shirt as I zipped up my zipper.

"I don't understand what you mean? Chill on what? Hanging out? Getting blazed? Hooking up? Really, Asher, what's going on?"

"The hooking up part?" I paused between each syllable making it sound more like a question. Teddy backed away, putting space between us as I redid my belt.

"What, did you find someone serious or something?"

"No, I just… I think what we do is fun. But we also have fun doing other stuff. I want to keep having fun…but maybe a little less…"

"Hooking up?" She finished my sentence. "Yeah."

She rolled her neck, holding her hands out on the offensive, and I swear she knew I was hiding something. "You know you can tell me if you have someone. I'm not going to be mad. Especially if you're trying to be on some exclusive shit."

"Teddy, you know I'm not trying to be on some exclusive shit with someone unless it's with you."

"So, what, you'd drop everyone in your phone to be in a relationship with me?"

I paused, and by the look on her face, she'd taken offense with how long it took me to answer. "Well, I'm not going to just do it if you're not on the other side waiting for me. That'd be stupid on my end."

"You're so full of shit."

"Teddy, while we're getting things out in the open…for you, I'd totally be the relationship type. I am the relationship type in the right situation. And I'd be everything you'd want me to be if that's what you asked of me. But I know you, Teddy, and I know Reggie—"

"Okay, so what does Reggie have to do with anything?" she interrupted.

As if she didn't already know. "C'mon, Ted, dude's feeling you like tenfold. I feel like I'm in the way of that."

Teddy rolled her eyes and collapsed on the couch. "What happened to, 'Oh, whatever we do is between you and me?'" she said in an unflattering imitation of what was supposed to sound like me.

"Well, I was talking to Reggie the other day—"

That was where I made my mistake. Teddy wasn't someone who I'd known to be a short fuse, but when things made her angry, she didn't stand down. She shot straight up, tense and less forgiving than the minutes prior.

"Wait, so you both were just talking about me?"

"No. Not like…not the way it sounds. You just came in his conversation. I listened, gave my opinion. That was all. It wasn't really a big thing."

By now she was pissed. "So, wait, so he brought me up? You

put in *your* two cents and now you're talking about backing out? Not going to lie, Asher, for someone claiming it wasn't a big thing, you two must have had a lot of to say."

Was she really this selfish? Or was it just an ego thing? Whatever I said now, she'd fight the idea just to be argumentative.

"So what are you trying to do? Cut me off? Not be friends? Because that's what the hell it sounds like—"

It probably wasn't the brightest idea to interrupt her, but she was putting her foot in her mouth. Only seeing things the way she saw them. Not considering anyone else's feelings.

"All right, Teddy, real talk…" I edged my lips into a smile, hoping doing so would change the mood. "So you know I'm, like, way into you, right? I feel like I'm catching feelings for you. Shit, I may even be in love with you. But I don't know if you feel the same way about me. The way I see it, the one risking the most here is me. Not you, not Reggie—me."

"Asher, you don't know shit about how I feel. You know how you don't know? Because you don't ask me."

I had my reasons why I didn't, but outside of being attracted to me, hanging out, and fucking, it didn't seem like there was much I needed to know.

"Okay, so tell me how you feel?"

"Asher, why tell you now? Doesn't make any sense seeing as how you're dropping me."

"Who says I'm dropping you? No one is saying we can't be friends anymore. We're cool. Like now. Hanging out, not ripping each other's clothes off. You don't have to tell me in words that Reggie's friendship is important to you, and I'm sure the two of you still hook up."

"Um, has *he* told you that?" she asked, getting angrier and angrier by the second.

"Well, no, not really. But c'mon, Teddy. I'm not stupid. Plus it's none of my business what the two of you do. It's cool, Teddy. The only thing that has to change is the intimacy. That's it."

"So let me see if I understand this. *You* and *Reggie* had a talk, and suddenly you've come to a decision about me? What say do I have in it at this point? Seems like you both of have already made up your minds. Tempted to just shut both of you out."

"What do you mean? You don't want to be cool or something?"

"Asher, what's the point? What's to stop you from saying next week, '*I don't want to be the one you smoke with*' or the week after that you tell me you don't want to go out to eat anymore."

"What? So because I don't want to be your fuck buddy, you want to just shut me out your life?"

She took out her phone, and her eyes widened in annoyance, clearly unwilling to answer my question.

"That's real fucked up, Teddy."

"Save it."

"I'm just saying, you're not going to find a whole ton of guys that want to be *just* your friend. That are going to listen to you without wanting something in return. It sounds fucked up, but it's true. I know I'm not perfect, but dammit, Teddy, I'm a good friend and I'm there for you. I want to keep being there for you but not *that* way, not while you're steady trying to figure out your feelings."

I picked up my hat and stood. Teddy, who not more than a minute ago refused to face me, turned her eyes in my direction.

"What, are you leaving now?"

"It's clear you don't want me here if you can't get your way. It's okay, Ted, I'm used to it. I don't even take offense to it anymore."

My feet felt made of metal as I dragged myself out of her apartment. She didn't stop me but I hadn't expected her to. The hardest thing about walking away *was* walking away. It hurt now, but in the long run, I considered myself lucky. If I kept on, nothing would stop what I had with Teddy from mentally and emotionally destroying me.

* * *

Teddy

Minutes. Hours. Days. That's how much time'd gone by since I'd last spoken to Asher. We'd both said some things in the heat of the moment, but where I wasn't ready to stand one hundred percent by my words, Asher seemed serious. What could I do to make things right?

There was something different, something special that drew me to both guys. Reggie and I had more time together. A blossom in spring that never fully bloomed. There was potential with him, but nothing I was eager to explore because we were both too stubborn to give in to what we wanted, even if it was at different times.

Asher was new, adventuresome. He made me feel alive, and for that reason he had me fucked up. As much as I hated to admit it, Asher was right. He'd been a good friend to me. Probably the best I've ever had. Losing him would be far more damaging than losing Reggie. But even if Reggie wasn't the person for me, I did treasure his friendship. When we actually acted like friends. I couldn't choose between them. I couldn't choose.

Knock-knock.

My text notification went off, and I threw myself over the couch to see who it was. Disappointment settled in when I realized it wasn't who I was expecting. I really wanted it to be Asher.

Wanted to talk for a sec...

Reggie. Triple friggin' sigh. Reggie always wanted to talk about something. There was never a point of our friendship where this guy didn't want to talk about something. Mostly himself, something I wasn't in a diehard rush to hear about.

I exhausted all my *Candy Crush* lives and tended to my *Farmville* crops and responsibilities before I replied back. A solid fifteen minutes in between text and reply. Short and vague. That's how I kept my answers. For all I knew, all he'd want to do is bring up nonsense that was only important to him. My thoughts flew back with what went down with Asher. Was this just another play on that?

Me: *About?*

I know it killed him that I didn't have an iPhone. That meant no way to predict when to expect my texts.

Reggie: *I've been thinking. We play a lot of games with each other. Ain't we a little too grown for games?*

Me: *Agreed. What's your point?*

There was a long pause before his reply. I prayed it wouldn't be some manifold of messages.

Reggie: *You know I'm feeling you. I know you're feeling me. There's so much damn bullshit out there, I'd rather just be with the one that makes me happy, even if she gets on my nerves. I can't take much more of these girls who lie upfront, using me for shit I don't have and acting like I owe them something because I think they're bad. We work well because you get me. And what you see is what you get with you and that's all I want...*

I rolled my eyes. So the guy went through some bad chicks. Join the club.

Teddy: *You get what you pay for. You don't have time, so you can't be mad que se comio el mojon.*

He hated when I texted in Spanish, especially when it wasn't things that could easily be translated.

Reggie: *Teddy, I'm trying to be an adult. I'm trying to be a man and just tell how I feel, make you see how serious I am about being serious about us.*

Me: *Okay.*

Reggie: *DAMN, JUST OKAY???*

Why did people text in bold letters? So damn annoying.

Teddy: *What is everybody nuts all of a sudden? Like seriously, you had months to come to this conclusion but you want me to give you an answer in a day. Okay so maybe you're "sure" now but now I'm not so "sure." Right now I'm not so sure about anything. Adding another headache...not on my list of things to do.*

Reggie: *It's a yes or no situation*

Teddy: *Cool, then right now it's a no*

Reggie: *No???*

Teddy: *I'm sorry...did you want me to lie?*

Reggie: *Teddy, I am not playing games with you anymore. I'm not like these other dudes out here. Do you want to have a real conversation about us or don't you?*

Teddy: *Well, when you put it like that, no, I don't.*

There was a short pause in between texts. Just when I thought he'd been done arguing.

Reggie: *Prolly over there with "homeboy"*

Teddy: *You're an assclown. Ever think homeboy was there for me when you didn't have "time"? Ever think I had needs that weren't being met but always ignored them just so we could chill? Ever think I have problems that don't have anything to do with you? Everything is always about you, you, you. If that's what you have planned for us, I'm good. I don't deserve everything, but I deserve more than that. I have no problem bowing out, don't like it? Have a nice life.*

CHAPTER THIRTEEN

Asher

I wonder if growing up, my favorite word had been "and". Whenever I spoke to my niece Mimi over the phone, it seemed like the word she used best. Every sentence ended in "and." It was like *The NeverEnding Story*.

Even when I was in the crappiest of moods, her voice had the ability to put me in a better one, which was necessary when it came to my sister Logan. Even though we were eighteen months apart, we weren't the closest of siblings. We didn't click. Ever. Most times I couldn't even stand to be in the same room as her, but it slightly changed when she made me an uncle three years ago.

I kept the peace for Mimi because I didn't have any other siblings. I absolutely adored my niece. I wasn't ready for kids, but I got to vicariously live through my sister whenever Mimi was around. I didn't always have time to be the uncle I wanted, so whenever Mimi would *pretend* to dial my number by accident, I knew it was because Logan was trying to use her cuteness against me to ask me to watch her.

Mimi pronounced my name like "Ash-sure," something that always made me laugh and made it hard to say no when she was involved. She liked to talk so much, she told me nearly everything that happened to her since the last time I watched her. Mimi didn't even sound as if she wanted to get off the phone when Logan took it from her.

Decent mood heavily averted. We spent the next minute arguing on whether I'd do it *this* morning, not a high priority on my to-do list. I agreed because she didn't have anyone else. Our parents were weirdos, and her taste in dudes was why she didn't have anyone to watch her in the first place. God forbid the woman ever say thank you. I love spending my entire morning before work watching your daughter.

Which with Mimi, I kind of did. But Logan always had an attitude about everything.

I had a few hours until I left, so when Reggie's number came up on my phone screen, I figured it couldn't be important.

"Yo." The most formal greeting Reggie would get answering the phone.

"You work today?"

"Yeah, what's up?"

Reggie spent three minutes trying to convince me to meet up with him to score his weed for him. I wasn't ashamed that I smoked, but I wasn't about to expose that to my niece. If her mother ever found out, I'd never hear the end of it. Plus, I had a level of respect for my sister and niece and helping a friend out would pretty much cross that line, so I made it clear I couldn't help him. At least not right now.

He hung up the phone disappointed, but I'm sure he'd find someone else to score it for him. I knew at least one person he could ask.

* * *

It was barely nine o' clock when I got home from work. Sundays were usually the slowest day of the week, so the workload made it so I was out early. With the repairs done on my bike, I was home in fifteen minutes, especially since the traffic was good. I thought about going out. It felt like one of those low moments, where nothing you did made sense until you were high. But I was opening in the morning, so I couldn't afford to oversleep.

When I was this bored, I usually masturbated, but I took one look at my dresser and decided against it. My dresser'd become my new bookcase. I didn't read for fun—mainly when I got bored —and there was absolutely nothing I could think up better to do with my time.

There were a total of two books sitting out, even though I owned three in total. It was the most I'd owned my entire life. They were all suggestions from Teddy, who I wouldn't be getting recommendations from anytime soon. But I'd read two in the weeks that passed, and it seemed like the best time to crack open the last one.

And Teddy thought *I* was dark. This stuff was some pretty heavy shit. I almost felt like I *was* high after starting one. I can't say I got into every one. The first book was good. I don't think I was its target audience, but I think even a non-geek could've dug it. The second book was just okay. Some of the details took me out the story too much, but for the second book I'd ever read that I wasn't forced to, it was decent.

I could've sworn I had three. I poked my head underneath the bed and found only a pile of dirty clothes. My room wasn't the cleanest, but I would've noticed a book out of place. I lifted up piles of clothes everywhere, pillows, random items I couldn't remember why they're there, and found nothing. This is why I *didn't* read. The cosmos would not allow it. Every force in the world told me I had better things to do.

But I didn't have better shit to do. I tore my room apart looking for that damn book. Even asked my roommates if they'd seen it lying around, as if they'd tell me if they actually did. The only other place I could've left it was Teddy's place. I hadn't talked or texted her since she'd let it be known she wasn't interested in a friendship she didn't call the shots for.

I wasn't sweating it…much. But if I asked her and she didn't have it, she'd think I was thirsty. Or playing games. I hadn't deleted her number, but never using it was the same thing. She'd either tell me she had it or didn't. End of story.

Me: *Sry to text, but I didn't leave a book over there, did I?*

I didn't expect a reply. She was stubborn and hypocritical and a bunch of other things, so it surprised me when I got a reply not long after.

Teddy: *I have two Dawns, so prolly. My bad. Thought it was mine. On my bookshelf.*

I didn't want to make trouble for myself, so I dropped it there.

Me: *I guess keep it. Will just get another…*

I was about to put my phone in the charger when she texted me back, an all-time record for her. Two texts in five seconds. Wonder what the occasion was.

Teddy: *Why would I want two of the same book? You can get it. Unless you just don't want…*

Me: *I want. It's just…boundaries*

Teddy: *Either you want it or not. If it were my shit, I'd already be over your house…*

Me: *So I can swing by?*

Teddy: *Tonight?*

Me: *Not tonight, unless that's okay…*

I was bored anyway, but it was almost twenty past nine and I didn't want to give the wrong idea.

Teddy: *Tonight is cool. Now would be better, just in case I fall asleep. But it's up to you.*

Me: *Be there in a few.*

* * *

The water over by Teddy's way brought a chill to the humid, cool Miami night. A jacket wasn't necessary this late, but even eighty-degree weather felt like sixty with wind on your face. I parked and secured my bike on a sidewalk space and made my way to Teddy's condo entrance.

She was expecting me, so when I rang the doorbell, she buzzed me up without asking. I *almost* walked by the elevator until I noticed it was fixed. Maybe I'd be in and out after all. A twenty-second elevator ride led to a short stroll down her floor's hallway. A muffled "come in" was all that came from knocking on her front door.

When I walked in her apartment, it was hard to ignore the smell. Definitely weed. Fruitier, but not quite. Most likely a hybrid strain, but definitely more my taste as opposed to Teddy's.

"Damn, you got it nice in here," I said, attempting to lighten the mood. I didn't know what type of Teddy to expect from texts alone. She just sat on her couch, nursing a joint, pointing to the book on her coffee table.

I slid the book from the table to my hand and was about to book until she held out her hand and offered me a puff. I shouldn't have, but come on? To turn it down now would've been rude.

It was best not to make myself comfortable, so I sat on the opposite arm. I took the smoke from her small hands, inviting the hit. Inhaling the smoke was on point. I offered it back, but she turned it down.

"It's okay. I'm just going through stuff, but didn't want enough to fall asleep."

I hadn't seen Teddy in weeks. Four to be exact. It was a surprise she was okay with me being here, even if it was just to pick up something I'd left. She rubbed the space between her eyes and curled her legs on the couch cushions.

"You okay?"

Teddy hid behind a forced smile and buried her face into her forearm. "Yeah. I'm just on my chemo weeks, and I have three days until my next rest, so…yeah."

"That sucks." She rubbed the area between her chest and neck, and I noticed. "You sure you okay?"

"Just a little sore." Sometimes she covered it with gauze. Most times by the time I saw her, it was partly healed. By now the spot where her Hickman line was looked raw, and her body language didn't hide that. Now I felt bad leaving her by herself. I handed her back the joint, and she smoked the rest and put it out. "Do you want to talk about it?"

She laughed a silent laugh and stretched out over the couch. "Asher, you're like the only person that ever asks me that anymore. I haven't seen you or Reggie in, like, forever. And you *still* ask me that."

It'd never been my business and I didn't want to know, but the moment she mentioned Reggie, I was curious. Reggie didn't discuss her, therefore I didn't. Backing out had only been for Teddy to figure out her feelings. Knowing that she hadn't talked to either of us made me wonder whether it'd been worth it. What was the month free of Teddy for if they weren't even speaking?

"You're telling me you haven't spoken to either of us since then?"

"Gosh, don't you guys talk to each other? You talk about *everything* else," she spit with venom, even if it wasn't intentional.

"And say what? '*Hey, Reg, me and Teddy stopped hooking up. All yours*'? "

Teddy rolled her eyes, shifting onto the couch, which didn't look comfortable but must've been to her. "You don't have to be sarcastic. It's not like I ever really knew what that was about anyway. You guys just blindsided me. First, you tell me some bullshit, which for the record, I haven't been around just you. But that doesn't mean I've been with Reggie. Sexually, at least. And you say something while I'm high on morphine and you come at me all types of weird. Then I'm getting from Reggie we're not cool anymore unless I'm willing to be his girlfriend. So, yeah, I haven't talked to either of you."

"Damn."

"Don't act so disappointed. I'm sure you didn't miss me much. Probably plenty of backups in that phone of yours."

Sure, my phone wasn't dry, but I wasn't swimming in sex either. "I'm not a robot, Teddy. What do you think I'm capable in a month?" I wasn't about to get sentimental, but I did genuinely miss Teddy's company. In addition to the sex.

"Don't play good boy with me," she said, curling her lips into a smirk. "I have a hard time believing you're a quality-over-quantity type of guy."

"To be honest, I'm an *any* type of guy. But you're misreading me. I'm not out replacing people like it's something to do."

"It's not like I am either. It's just...I'm dealing with enough. Dealing with you used to be easy. Once dealing with you two became harder, even as friends—"

"I get it. You have to do you."

"The only thing that sucks about it though..." She started the sentence but left it open-ended.

"What?"

"Nothing." She shooed her hand at me. "You'll just think I'm baiting you."

"I'm pretty sure I'm grown enough to get shit. You don't have to slow anything down for me."

Teddy shifted, leaning on her elbow. She held out her palms defensively at me before she continued on. "Just don't think I'm purposely trying to wrap your mind around it. I'm only saying it because you asked."

"Just say it."

"You eat way better pussy than anyone I've been with. I feel like I have to masturbate to orgasm that easy. There's like, people so whack I don't even know why their numbers are still in my phone." She laughed, taking it as a joke.

"If you were seriously trying to silence the room, you could've left it as, 'You eat way better pussy' and I would've had complete understanding."

That comment generated a laugh from Teddy, the first genuine one all night. "I wasn't trying to throw it out there. I'm just saying because you asked. I know you have better things to do than to hear me complain, so I'm not trying to keep you."

I sat up for the first time since I got there, book in tow. "Wish I could help you with that issue, but we're, like, not cool like that anymore," I said with a shrug. "Seeing how I stepped aside and you're not even *talking* to Reggie, I would've totally licked your pussy. Because that's the kind of friend that I am." I turned on my heel, just a few inches from the door before I stopped to add. "And I wouldn't have asked for anything. Because…you know?"

Sparking intimacy up so soon after her treatment rarely happened between us, but she never wanted to so I was cool with it. I didn't even know if she could.

"Just shut up, Asher, and c'mere."

I rejoined Teddy on the couch, and she crawled over to me and straddled my lap. "I'm assuming you want to take me up on my offer?"

She inched closer to me, pressing her lips to mine. I didn't put much force, but I held her hips and pulled her closer.

"I miss you as a friend. I miss doing stuff with you. Doing stuff to you. You doing stuff to me. All I wanted was a little heads up. And for it to be something *you* want. Not something you think I want," She said, spending half the time with her lips against mine, the other half trying to speak.

"Mmm…I missed you."

"Show me how much you missed me." Like that, I was sucked back in Teddy's web. She could've bit my head off, but nothing would've made me less whole in that moment.

* * *

I was beyond defeated, and by the looks of it, Teddy was, too. Teddy's body wasn't doing what she wanted it to, and I was frustrated she kept pretending it was. Oral sex wasn't eliciting a response, even the techniques she usually went nuts over. When I asked if she was close, she confessed chemo sometimes affected her sex drive and that it wasn't as easy to orgasm so soon afterward.

"It's not like I can't. It's just... Maybe we should just do it. It might be easier to come once you're inside me." Teddy pointed out the condoms in her dresser, only moments separated me from slipping one on and sliding inside her. Her body felt familiar but gave me a fight I wasn't used to. One of her ankles went to my ear, the other leg rested against my waist. I took my time, watching each pained reaction to each thrust.

"Teddy, talk to me. Tell me what I'm doing wrong."

She leaned her body up and reached for a bottle of lube, recalling all the fun times we had when we used it. I paid extra attention to the outside of the condom, but made sure to rub it all over and inside her, too. She winced as my fingers explored and massaged inside of her, preparing her to make room for me.

"You don't look like you're having fun."

"I'm okay. Just...go slow this time."

I nodded and kneeled in front of her, resting my hips between her thighs. I slid inside her, mixing the cool slickness of the condom with the warmth of her body. She felt better and easier this time, but it didn't stop the wry faces she wore, out of pain. Not pleasure.

"Teddy, this isn't working."

"We can keep going if you're close."

"Teddy it's making me soft just watching you." I pulled out, lying next to her on the bed. I pulled off the condom and watched her hide her face against her pillow to muffle her crying.

"We don't have to do anything," I said, kissing the back of her neck and shoulders. The skin was so soft there, it didn't matter that it wasn't her lips. "Really. It's okay," I repeated, but it was always hard to calm a person down once they got to that point.

I wasn't big on crying. Not for any reason other than I didn't find much to cry about. But I knew it was just better to do it, than to fight it. I wrapped my arms around Teddy and waited for her moment to pass, occasionally drawing kisses along the back of her shoulders. When my hand got bored, I rubbed the skin above her navel, marking territory with each inch until I had a handful of her breast. As long as my touch didn't hurt, my hands made all the expeditions she'd allow.

I licked my index finger and thumb and teased the nipple that was available to me. Her back arched to me as a lengthy gasp followed. I leaned over her, bringing her tit closer to my mouth to give it the attention it deserved. She rested her hand on my chin, pushing me up to kiss her mouth.

Slow, gentle, sensual kisses. On anyone else, it would've left me wanting more. Every time *she* claimed my lips, I didn't need more. Any kiss was enough. My hands kept busy, my lips were on hers, her moans vibrating against my lips.

"That feel good?" I whispered between kisses, even though she was too busy to answer.

Her fingers gently dragged across my face, and she asked if I could switch sides on the bed. Leaning on her right side was easier, and she just wanted to kiss face-to-face. A little maneuvering on the bed, and we were body-to-body, lip-to-lip, and—when I wanted to tease her—mouth-to-tit.

Having her hard nipples between my lips made me hard as fuck. I relied on her hike in breaths to tell me whether she liked the difference from how I licked and sucked. Playing with her breasts was always fun, but I'd definitely stepped my game up, knowing how responsive she was to it, even when the rest of her body wasn't. Her hand slid down to touch me, feel me, caress my hard-as-hell cock.

"You're really hard," she moaned back to me.

"That's because your tits are fucking amazing."

She held my face and willed it back to hers, and we greeted each other with sloppy, drugged kisses. She brought tinges of pleasure as her hands brushed against my stomach, until they rubbed the inside of my thighs. If she was trying to torture me, it was working. Each finger felt like individual silk, slow and sensual, with just enough time to enjoy the touch.

When she leaned up, I thought she was about to give me head, but she reached for the lube instead, drenching her hands in it. Her fingers slid over my cock, and I prepared myself for minutes of yanking and pulling, the "go-to" for most girls who had no idea how to give a decent hand job. I hated to come that way, but I didn't complain. The fact she cared meant more than *how* I got there.

She switched things up when she brought both hands to my dick, using one to caress my shaft, the other to stimulate the head, proving now that my body wasn't ready for that type of excitement. My hands balled fistfuls of her sheet, watching her hands take turns stroking the different lengths of my cock.

"Damn, Teddy, is there anything you don't know how to do?" I said in short, silted breaths. She was too far for me to touch her, but the visual of her naked body definitely added to fantasy.

Her hands alternated between twisting slowly in an opposite direction and massaging the length of my cock with one hand, her fingers forming a cock ring with the other. She knew just the right pressure to handle me with, so it didn't feel that much different from her mouth. When she let go of the head, she massaged the skin where the shaft and head met. I gasped, begging her not to stop. My body let go of its tension, surrendering to the sweet euphoria of her touch.

"God, Teddy. That felt amazing."

The aftermath was all over her hands, streaming down the length of me. She didn't waste time wiping down the mess with a towel, handing it back to me when she was down. I held my arms out as she collapsed on my chest. I planted light kisses on her forehead, still high off the feeling.

"I love you."

But she was already asleep. I kissed her forehead one more time and slipped out of bed to gather up my clothes. I covered her body with the sheet and kissed the exposed skin of her shoulders. She perked up to the touch and slightly opened her eyes.

"Teddy, I have to go. I didn't want you to think I just left."

She nodded, curling back into her covers.

A girl like her—she was worth losing sleep over.

CHAPTER FOURTEEN

Teddy

I searched through my closet for something easy and loose-fitted to wear, unable to decide between a pair of baggy sweatpants or a comfy pair of old school track pants that made loud swishing sounds whenever you took a step. I didn't remember where they'd come from. All I knew was they were there and felt so weightless that I'd almost forget I had them on—that is, until I walked. They were so damn comfy I was almost willing to take the risk.

I was told not to eat anything for six hours before my scheduled PET scan, which was hard since the morning was when I was my hungriest. I'd go another two or three hours without food once I arrived at the imaging center, and I was super bummed that the only thing I *was* allowed to consume was water. Plain water—no sugar, no sweeteners, no caffeine. A total nightmare if you asked me since I had a major inkling for Starbucks. Once I left that place, I was getting a venti for the hell of it and the biggest, unhealthiest burger I could find. Enduring months of this mess, I was expecting some good news thrown my way.

My phone buzzed with a text, and I rushed to the bed to see who it was from. Just the person I wanted to hear from. Asher.

Asher: *Let me know how everything goes today. We can go out later if you're up for it. Wanted to talk about doing something for Valentine's Day...*

That's right. With everything that'd been going on, it'd slipped my mind that it was just a few days from now. I was never big on cheesy holidays, Valentine's Day being the cheesiest of them all. But this year I actually had someone who threw the offer out there to do something. Even if we were only going as friends that had sex, I knew he would take the time to make it sweet and special. He was corny like that.

Me: *What did you plan on doing for Valentine's Day?*

Asher: *You :)*

I laughed into my phone.

Me: *Dumbass. Really, tell me*

Asher: *You know shit like that is supposed to be a surprise*

Me: *Damn I hope you don't plan on going all out...*

Which was basically my way of saying I hoped he planned on going all out.

Asher: *Don't worry about all that. Just be patient and don't make any plans that day. Had a few things in mind. Down?*

Teddy: *Dress code?*

It took him a few minutes to text back, but when he did, it was a picture message. It was a full-length photo taken in front of his mirror, wearing something I'd never seen him in before—a tailored suit with a red silk tie. I wouldn't have believed he could pull that look off had I not seen it with my own eyes, but now that my eyes were open, I looked forward to peeling him out of every piece.

Asher: *Te gusta?*

I smiled. Him and his non-speaking-Spanish ass.

Teddy: *Si, eso es me gusta! Y tu pelo? Te vas a peinar sola?*

He texted back.

Asher: *Baby steps, Teddy. Baby steps, lol. But yeah wear something sexy. For you, I can't imagine that being hard.*

I was just about to reply, when another message came up.

Asher: *Or you can just come naked and I'll improvise.*

Teddy: *Just dumb*

Asher: *But really, later. Hit me up if you're up for it. I want to see you, dummy.*

Teddy: *Have to get going. Maybe see you then.*

Asher: *Good luck.*

Asher didn't have a lot of knowledge of PET scans, but by now I was a pro. I didn't need luck. What I needed was food.

* * *

I checked into the imaging center an hour before my scheduled time. Naiveté always made me think that, by coming early, they'd in turn take me early. It didn't work that way. Even if all my paperwork was filled out and turned in, I was always seen right on the dot.

The technologist called me in and guided me through the hallways to one of the waiting rooms. She was a young woman, no more than five years older than me. Perhaps it was her short pixie cut or maybe even her fuller figure, but I liked her. She was warm and welcoming, not at all stuffy like the technologists I'd met with before.

She handed me a hospital gown and excused herself for me to get ready, which didn't take me long. As I laid down on the hospital bed, she explained the next few things that were going to take place. Steps I already had knowledge of, this being my third PET this year, but I supposed it was to make me aware of everything that was going on and make me feel at ease. Her soothing voice helped with that.

She tied a thick rubber strap above my forearm as she examined my arm for the right vein. "You aren't needle shy, are you? I always ask folks before I start the intravenous line."

I shook my head. If I wasn't used to needles by now there was something seriously wrong with me. Could never prepare myself for that first prick, though. It always stung like hell.

"So now I'm going to check your blood sugar levels, and once that's all set, I'm going to go ahead and start with the radiotracer component. As you know, it takes about forty-five minutes to an hour to work its way through your system, so feel free to entertain yourself with any reading materials you have or music while you wait. Once I take you to the scanning area, I'd advise you to leave your things behind. I promise, *promise* once I get you in the machine, I'll have you out of here in an hour or so."

I tried to think of sliding into this tubular hole as living in a space opera, where the machine wasn't a detector of how my tissues and organs worked but instead a bed I slept in one of those outer space communities. I hadn't read a lot of space operas, but whenever they described their living quarters, I imagined them no different than this cramped-ass scanner.

What was I going to wear for Valentine's Day? I had this little black dress I'd bought a few months ago, but I think I'd need shapewear to wear it. When I'd first bought it, it'd fit me just right, but since then I'd put on a few pounds (thank god) so now it was tight on me. The thought crossed my mind that I should probably be corny and wear something red to match Asher's tie, but I had nothing in red I wanted to wear, so I guess I'd be hitting up the mall after this.

Conversations with myself was how I spent the rest of the hour. Before I knew it, I was sliding out of the tube, and the technologist helped me off the examining table. She made a few light jokes as she guided me back to the room with all my clothes and gadgets.

"Once we get this off to the radiology unit, we should have your results in about two days, give or take. Make sure once you leave you drink lots of fluids to help flush the component out of your system. Don't skim on the water."

I smiled weakly. "Thanks."

"You should be all set, Ms. King. Let me give you a few moments to yourself to get dressed, and then I'll walk you out. In the meantime, if you have any questions, feel free to ask when I come back to check on you."

The only question I had was where the closest place to stuff my face.

* * *

I meant to call Asher with an update when I was out of my PET scan, but I was starving. A phone call to him was going to have to wait. I knew he'd understand. The guy ate like, every four hours and couldn't imagine going without food as long as I had. If I didn't get something in my stomach now I was going to faint.

I pulled into my local Starbucks and waited in line, silently debating what kind of coffee I should get. The refreshers seemed to call me, but I'd waited all day to get some caffeine. I went with a venti Caramel Brulée latte and was warned that this would be the last week they'd be serving it. Bummer since it was my favorite. I walked out to my car to see an oversized plush red and white unicorn sitting on the hood of my convertible. It was super corny, but it had to be from Asher. It just had to be.

I ran over and opened the card attached to its neck, reading the contents aloud to myself. "Turn around."

This was so sweet. I couldn't wait to cover him in kisses. I spun around and felt a wave of disappointment. Standing in front of me was someone I hadn't seen—or even wanted to see—in weeks. Reggie. I mumbled a quick *fuck,* but it was too late. He was on his way over.

He had a bouquet of roses in one hand and a big red envelope in the other. He reached in and gave me a hug, and while I wasn't particularly interested in anything he had to say, he was never someone I'd considered to be a big spender. Something about his job always cutting his hours or something.

"Um, how did you know I'd be here?"

"I didn't. But I was buying this stuff for Valentine's Day and said, hell, let me stop by Starbucks while I'm over here. And what were the odds I'd see your car? So I said fuck it. Why wait for the fourteenth to surprise you. Surprise."

I was surprised all right.

He handed me the flowers and pestered me until I opened the card. Whimsical typography jumped out at me as a cute baby turtle rushed off to its corner street mailbox.

I made sure to send all my friends a valentine, starting from the plainest to the most beautiful. You were my last one.

I laughed at how cheesy it was and the fact that it provoked a smile out of me. "You're so whack for this, Reggie. Seriously."

"But you like it, though, right?"

A laugh came through despite me forcing a frown. "I like the unicorn. The flowers…they're a bit much. You know I don't like flowers." But he didn't know that. He didn't know a lot about me and that was because he rarely thought to ask. Asher always asked.

"Fuck, Teddy, I miss you. And I want to take you out on Valentine's Day. I mean, unless *homeboy* is planning something."

I knew where this was headed. He was trying to be nosy and get me to talk. This coming from the same person that'd given me an ultimatum that if I didn't take him seriously, then there was nothing we could offer each other. Which I was fine with, but I hated when people went back on their word. This was a clear case of that.

"Reggie, why do you care?"

"Teddy, first of all, you haven't seen me in a long time. Give me some kind of credit. I'm trying to prove to you that I'm more serious than that other dude."

I rolled my eyes out of aggravation. "I have to go."

He grabbed my arm just as I opened the door to my car. "Can I at least treat you to some food and a good time?"

"Define good time?"

* * *

Tonight was the first time in a long time I was able to kick back and enjoy myself with Reggie. We devoured a massive amount of bar food and played round after round of *HillBilly Shootout*. Amusement centers were a blast when you were with the right person. Reggie was definitely the right person for this tomfoolery.

He challenged me to a game of *Hit 'Em Hoops*, but I sucked, so I didn't score many baskets. The little kids running around this place were getting on my last nerve, and ever since we'd given a kid two hundred of the tickets we won, he was basically stalking us to fork up the rest. I was ready to go anyway. Asher was waiting on my call and I had to drop Reggie off at home ASAP.

Spanish pop blared from my stereo as Reggie adjusted the volume to a lower level, taking me out of the zone.

"Have a good time tonight?"

I had half a mind to lie, but what would it hurt if I told him the truth? I did have fun, especially without the pressure of being anything more.

"Yeah, tonight was cool, Reg. Thanks for the night out."

He put his hand on my clothed thigh, but I quickly pried it off and placed it back on his lap. "Watch it, Reg. It wasn't *that* good of a time."

"Teddy, it's like I haven't seen you in forever. I miss you. Calling you. Texting you. Amongst other things. I know you had to have missed me too, even if it's just a little."

It was true. The reason Reggie and I worked was because there'd been a time we were on the same wavelength. We hadn't expected much from each other, and when we'd realized that, we were at our height. Now that he wanted something serious with me, he was a thorn in my side, una avispa buzzing in my ear. His friendship, though. I really missed calling him my friend.

"I miss you. But just a little. It's more I miss your corny-ass jokes," I teased.

"So let me take you out for V-Day. I promise to be whack all night."

It was hard keeping my eyes on the road when Reggie was being so stupid. Thankfully, I pulled up to his house in peace.

"Today was fun, but to say we'll hang on Valentine's Day is something I can't promise you. I'm sorry."

He made a sour face and pouted his lips like a sad-ass little puppy. "Well, at least let me treat you to a quick session. I know I have to owe you, like, nine."

In all my history with Reggie, there'd never been a time where he was *this* generous. First the gifts, then dinner, and now this? The next thing I expected was for it to snow in Miami. I unbuckled my seatbelt.

"Just because you're in a giving mood. I only have a few minutes to chill, but if I get downstairs and you try to play me, I'm leaving."

His grandmother's car was missing from the driveway, so I knew that was the only reason he asked me down. His grams had no problem if he indulged himself, but if I was there, I was the reason he smoked "that stuff." Some women just couldn't see their sons (or grandsons) as they were.

I followed him to the basement and almost lost my shit when my eyes settled on what was in front of me. Felt pink and red arrows led down the steps to his bed as cheesy soft music played in the background. Pink and white rose petals formed the silhouette of a gigantic heart on his red satin sheets. Mind blown.

"Um…this is really nice, Reggie. I hope all this isn't for me?"

Reggie trailed behind me down the stairs, but I was too

surprised to catch his expression. "Well, it isn't for my grandmother."

I stopped at the end of the staircase to examine the safest part in the room to sit. "I told you, Reggie, if you try to play me—"

"Girl, will you relax? Damn. I set this up thinking we'd be chilling for Valentine's Day. How was I supposed to know I'd run into you? It's not even done anyway. You're welcome to ignore everything. If you're just trying to be out, it'd take me forever to take this shit down."

I couldn't blame Reggie for trying. Had this gesture been used three months ago, I might've reconsidered. But I was here for a session and a session only. I decided the couch was the least suggestive place to sit. Reggie's bed full of petals was a bit overkill, and even though the couch had a velveteen throw for the occasion, it was much less mushy.

Besides, the A/C was blaring down here. The throw would be just enough to defend myself against the chill. I almost hoped Reggie had some other chick he could call up. With all the effort, it'd be such a shame to waste it.

Whether he'd rolled it in the time I'd been here or ahead of time, he handed me a joint that was already ready to blaze. I sniffed it to examine the aroma, and with its heavy pine smell, it was definitely kush. Reggie offered me the first puff, burning the end to get things going, and I offered it back.

I missed Indica. Whenever I got high with Asher, he liked that higher-than-high feel, so sativa strains were usually what he brought. But I liked the lax feel of kush. I felt like a melting ice cream cone on it.

"Remember that time we dined and ditched that restaurant—" Reggie started in a high state. Even as he went on to tell the full story and I cackled and repeated some moments verbatim with him, it wasn't exactly how he remembered.

Technically *he* dined and ditched. We waited over twenty minutes at a diner for waiters who outright ignored us. It wasn't until someone was new on shift took our order, but by then we were so pissed, we planned on running out on the bill. The waitress seemed too good for that place, catering to our every request. When I went to the bathroom and heard an exchange between her and an employee about her accent and how it was "America" so she should learn better English, I didn't have the heart to stiff her like that.

Reggie'd already bounced, assuming my trip to the bathroom resulted in ditching through an emergency exit. But I made sure the bill was paid in full, with a ten-dollar tip. It wasn't much when you're a waitress, but she appreciated it more than some of the other stuck-up waitresses would have. I held up the lie when I met Reg at my car, and to this day, he still thinks we dined and ditched.

So I'd been keeping *three* things from him.

We bullshitted about some other old times that ended in a conversation about our sex life—or, rather, lack of one. We'd had some good times, but it surprised him that I'd gotten up with women, too, because he figured I'd said things like that in the past just to say it. Who says that just to say it?

"You know how girls be saying that just to get dudes to think about it?"

As if everything I did was for a male gaze.

At least we were even cool enough to have conversations like that. Guys were so protective over who they slept with. He'd been the only guy outside of Ash I'd ever messed with that didn't slut shame me for having needs. I can't say whether it would've been different if I'd actually been his girlfriend, but since we'd never been more than this, he did get me. Even if it were only half the time.

Everything felt so calm at this point. Reggie stopped talking, but his snores gave him away. Dude was laid out. It made me jealous I wasn't in my own bed. I curled up on the couch and closed my eyes. I thought I'd just rest them, but when I opened them again, it was nearly four in the morning.

Reggie's grandmother held an overnight position at a call center. She usually got home by six, and I wasn't trying to be there when she did. I caught a quick glance at Reg, and he'd barely moved from his spot. I left a text letting him know I'd call him and did my best to avoid the creaky steps to make my way to the first floor. Last night had been fun, but it was time to go.

CHAPTER FIFTEEN

Teddy

Payday had come with bells on and sirens. Every dollar of this check I was spending on enough candy to rot Teddy's teeth and was proud of myself for securing last-minute reservations at some five-star restaurant where even the appetizers started at thirty bucks. I'd spent so much money on these threads and wanted a place nice enough to wear it to. I wasn't the suit-and-tie type of guy, but Teddy had a rough couple of months and I wanted to show her how glad I was to have her back in my circle again, even if the lines weren't perfectly clear between us. That and I wanted to see her in something short, tight, and sexy. This suit was paying for itself in more ways than one.

There was something about this V-Day that made me hopeful for what the future looked like for us. We took things a day at a time and didn't force anything to happen that wasn't in the cards, but I was ready to call Teddy someone more than just my friend and I planned on making it the night to do so.

I was willing to accept that, while I dug being with her, she equally got on my nerves, but that was the thing about having feelings for someone. If it was great all the time, there wasn't enough substance in it for me. I needed someone who pushed my buttons as much as I wanted someone that made me happy. Teddy was that person.

My phone buzzed, and I knew from the ringtone that it couldn't be anyone but Reggie. He was that predictable.

"Sup?" I answered.

"What's good? You sound busy."

If busy sounded like I was laying down on my ass and talking to him. "I'm not. You caught me at a good time."

"Cool. I need to re-up. A little help please."

I got up and threw some pants on, as well as some slip-on canvas shoes. "Just beep when you're outside."

He beeped the horn a second later, and I looked outside my blinds.

"Dude, really?"

"I was in the neighborhood." *This guy.*

* * *

It was hard not to tell when Reggie was in a good mood. Dude had like three go-to emotions I experienced on a regular basis. Grumpy, grumpier, and "talk-me-off-a-cliff." Today was different. Either he got some or he'd stumbled across some extra cash. He'd splurged on a whole O and promised to hit me up with a third. Even I couldn't be in a mood that good.

"Damn, son. What's got you in a good-ass mood? I'm saying, Reggie, pass that."

He tossed his phone between his hands. "I just had a good night with Teddy, that's all. Shit, *more* than a good night."

My heart stopped. Did he just say what I think he did? "Wait, you mean you chilled with Teddy last night?"

I'd been trying to call her all night but hadn't been able to get a hold of her. Thought maybe she hadn't felt up to hang. Now I at least knew what happened.

"It was nice. Probably like the first time ever we didn't argue. We went out. We had fun. We got back to my place and one thing led to another. I swear if I could put together the perfect moment, it still wouldn't have been better than last night. I wanted to take her out for Valentine's Day, but I don't know, she was saying she had something going on with this guy she's been messing with. All I know is I bought a whole bunch of roses, lit some candles, and made last night better than homeboy could've ever made it."

He went on to tell me about how he had his room looking like a honeymoon suite, but all I seemed to focus on was the fact that last night Teddy chose him over me. What did I expect? Since the moment I'd met Teddy, she'd never seemed to make up her mind on what she wanted. This situation? More than enough made up my mind for me.

* * *

Teddy swung by at seven, but what with what I'd learned earlier, I didn't bother getting dressed. She had the top to her convertible up, and when I got in on the passenger side, I saw why. Her hair was different. Not curly, not straight. Bouncy, maybe? When she didn't want to mess her hair up, she always rode with the top up.

A flesh-toned, mid-length dress hugged her body in the most provocative way, leaving no mystery to all her dips and curves. A pang of regret ran through me as I debated going through what I'd planned to say to her. I should've postponed it. The way she looked tonight definitely called for a deferral, but the longer I wasted time, the longer it took to get my answers.

"Um, it's seven o'clock. Why aren't you dressed? I spent three hours at the Dominicans for my hair to look like this. The least you could be was ready."

I placed a gift bag of things I was going to surprise her with on the seat, but it didn't seem as important as asking her about last night.

"Hey, were you with Reggie last night?"

Her smile faded. I saw this going one of two ways. Either she'd lie, which would make zero sense since I knew already, or she'd tell me the truth.

"Yeah, about that. It was only supposed to be for a few minutes. I meant to call but I left my phone in the car. Time just flew after that. My bad."

At least she didn't lie.

"You know, Teddy, I try and try, but it's like no matter how much I try, I'm always going to compete with someone when it comes to you. The one thing I won't be in competition with is Reggie. He's my friend. You're my friend. But the thing is, you don't get to have it your way with the both of us. Not while I'm strong enough to walk away. Guess you can tell Reggie the better man won."

She called out as I exited her car, and a series of texts filled up my inbox as I walked to my front door.

Teddy: *I don't know what Reggie told you, but we didn't do anything. Just smoked, that's it!*

Me: *You don't have to explain anything to me. We're just friends. If you'd rather spend your V-Day with Reg, not gonna stand in your way. Just don't wanna be dragged into the web of games.*

Teddy: *Why are you being an asshole?*

Me: *I'm being honest. Anyways, hope you like the books I got you. I was reading somewhere that book geeks like you love first editions. No need to reciprocate, just thought of you when I found them. Happy V-Day.* ❤

I turned off my phone to silence the dozens of texts that followed. Tonight, I didn't want to deal with this.

CHAPTER SIXTEEN

Teddy

By the time I got home, I didn't even want to open the bag Ash gave me. What was the point now, right? He'd told me to basically fuck myself, so I should've just given the gift bag back to him. I was still curious, though. It was books—that much was obvious. Long and wide, like a grocery bag, but the paper inside hid its contents so well I had to indulge my curiosity if I ever wanted to know what was inside.

Shit.

First edition signed copies of *Wild Seed* and *Brown Girl in the Ring*. He knew they were two of my favorite books, but I already had them. It wasn't necessary to own two. He'd put a Post-it note inside the flap.

I hear book geeks like you like out-of-print first editions. Not sure I can cosign those signatures, though...

Sweet. I don't think anyone else I knew would've gone out of their way for something like this.

I pulled out a small box. My first guess was a shirt box, but it was too heavy to be clothes. I cracked open the side and spotted a furry pair of feet. I ripped the top off to find a smiling, dark brown bear in pajamas.

There was a birth certificate underneath with the name "Teddy King." The note with it was obviously from Ash.

Because one of you is not enough...

Was I supposed to feel worse than I did already? It's not like I hadn't wanted to spend my V-Day with Ash. He'd just heard one side of Reggie's story and gone with it and wasn't interested in hearing my end. There was one more gift at the bottom, but it was just a folded piece of paper. It could've been a gift certificate or a homemade card.

But when I unfolded the paper, it was just a simple note like the rest of them. I wish the words didn't cut into me the way they did. It was probably last to craft, first to go in. I'm surprised it hadn't gotten lost in the paper. I really did care about Ash. But even with just a sentence, the tone said it all.

Sometimes I just wish how I felt was enough...

I took my phone to call him. Every time it just went straight to voicemail, like he was screening my calls. Couldn't blame him since it's what *I* would do. I texted him, called him. I even left four voicemails—three nice versions of me until I got so irritated, the last one showed off my frustration.

"If you're just going to avoid me... I'm trying to say sorry but whatever."

My phone rang a few minutes after phone call four, and I picked it up before I confirmed who it was.

"Oh, now you pick up the phone?" I hid my face once I heard the Ukrainian accent over the phone. Oops.

It was just Zinc calling me with my PET scan results. I'd known him for so many years, he just laughed at my exchanges with him. I loved to get on his nerves, using my vernacular tenfold to make him know how it feels to hear him over the receiver.

"Theodora, I'm going to need you to sit if you're standing."

Weird. Sometimes he did that. Eastern European humor, I

guess. When he was convinced I was sitting down, he started speaking, and my mind went blank after his first sentence. Where was I? Why was he still talking? Was what he'd said even important?

I wasn't responding to chemotherapy.

I stood, and the phone slowly dropped from my ear and out of my hand, shattering into three pieces on the floor. *Just three.* I wondered…would it be that easy for me?

* * *

February 15th

Reggie: *Thought you were gonna call me? Fucked up. Guess "home-boy" had your time. It's okay though...*

February 16th

Asher: *Random: How'd you like the books?*

February 18th

Reggie: *Playing all these games. It's like you do this shit on purpose.*

February 20th

Asher: *You okay? Talked to Reggie. Thought you were avoiding me because you made your choice, but no one's heard from you in a week. You all right?*

February 22nd

Reggie: *Guess whatever*

February 24th

Asher: *Know I said a bunch of fucked-up shit but hope you're okay :/*

The texts kept coming in, and my interest to reply was at a minimum. Not only did I not need this shit right now, talking to either one of them would just make me feel worse than I already did. All I could worry about was me right now. What *I* was going to do, what choices *I* was going to make. Neither of those questions involved either one of them. I couldn't find a reason to text either of them back.

I didn't have an opinion right now. Everyone in on the situation was advising me what to do. Oncologists. Radiologists. Hematologists. My parents. I didn't have a say in what was going to happen at this point. It wasn't up for debate. I was going to treatment center in Minnesota. For how long, I didn't know.

I could always count on my cancer group to be supportive. No one was a stranger to outside help. Whenever a shoulder was needed, those who could meet, were there. I hoped they would always be there. There was never a time they didn't understand.

I wanted to talk to Asher. Would he even care if something bad happened to me? That was my greatest fear.

I wanted him to know. I wanted him to care.

* * *

Asher

Teddy: *I need to see you*

Five words. One text. It was the first text she'd replied to since our fallout, and while a part of me looked forward to knowing if she was all right, I also felt like it was another way of sucking me back into her world.

Maybe I'd been too harsh, unreasonable—hell, maybe even a little gullible—but I wanted her to know how she made me feel sometimes. Like shit. Every time she pulled me back in, it was only to spit me out. Maybe it was like a game to her, but I was all out of lives and tired of playing but decided once again, to go back.

Me: *What for?*

Maybe I could have used better wording.

Teddy: *Think what you want to... Truth is, I fell asleep over at his house and nothing else. If he told you anything more, it's not true.*

Me: *Okay...*

Teddy: *You know what? Fuck it. Take his word over mine. Results came back from my PET scan. Turns out I'm not responding to my treatments. You on some dumb shit isn't the worse news I've heard all week. Not interested in hearing from me? Peace out.*

My heart sank as I read her text. Not responding to her treatments. What the fuck did that mean? I read it over and over again as I threw on some clothes, waiting until I was outside walking to reply to her text.

Me: *OMG, tell me where you are...*

* * *

When I got to Teddy's place, she was sitting on a bench at a bus stop across the street from her condo. I hid behind a passive expression, a mix between contempt and disinterest, just in case this was just a ploy to get me here.

"Got here as soon as I could." I sat on the bench close to her and placed my hand at the small of her back. Tense, eager, and confused all in one. "Talk to me."

She turned to me, wiping tears away from her eyes. "Thanks for the books, Asher. I loved them," she sniffled. She had a small roller suitcase full of what I assumed was clothes. The teddy bear I'd given her the day before Valentine's Day peeked out the bag.

"Teddy, don't scare me like this. Tell me something. I came all this way."

She ran her hands down her face to wipe whatever new tears that formed. Her voice cracked when she finally spoke.

"My options are limited right now. The doctors told me my best options are with a clinical trial. The only clinical trial I qualify for is in Minnesota. And that's still not a guarantee it'll be effective. I've known for a week and a half now. Been sitting on it since then." Since the day before Valentine's. "With where the conversation went the last time we got up, I'm almost positive you don't care, but...I just wanted you to know."

A yellow taxi pulled up in front of us, and it was only now that everything she was telling me sunk in. She was leaving. She was leaving right now. And I'd been spending the past two weeks with no knowledge of how advanced things were or how long she'd be gone for. "Off to the airport," she said as she picked up her luggage and bag.

If only I'd gotten here a few minutes earlier, I could've apologized the proper way. I was speechless.

She stepped in front of me, pressing her fingers to her lips and then pressing her fingers to my mouth. Not satisfied with that, I pulled her in to kiss her and held her tight, like it might be the last time I'd see her.

"I don't care how you have to get in contact with me—call me, write me, email. Just don't leave me wondering how you are, Teddy."

She offered a soft, awkward smile and broke free from my embrace. I watched as the taxi drove off, without her so much as glancing at me outside her window. For the first time since she'd told me about her cancer, I was actually scared for her. Scared for myself. Scared for us.

I didn't want to think of this being the end of us.

I didn't want to think...

April 20th, 2016

Dear Asher,

Thank you for that...

Teddy

APRIL 13TH, 2016

DEAR TEDDY,

THIS IS LIKE, THE FIRST LETTER I'VE EVER WRITTEN. I TEXT SO

MUCH MY HANDWRITING LOOKS LIKE SHIT, SO I HOPE YOU CAN

READ IT XD

IT SUCKS THAT YOU'RE NOT DOING SO HOT. I WISH I COULD BE

THERE, JUST SO YOU'D HAVE SOMEONE TO TALK TO. YOU CAN

CALL ME ANYTIME. PHONES STILL WORK YOU KNOW?

ANYWAY, I KNOW YOU'LL BE BACK. FOR NOW, I WON'T

COMPLICATE THINGS MORE THAN THAT. JUST FOCUS ON

RECOVERY.

YOU'RE THE STRONGEST PERSON I KNOW. IF ANYONE CAN KICK

CANCER'S BUTT, IT'S YOU.

ASHER 

April 20th, 2016

Dear Asher,

Thank you for that...

Teddy

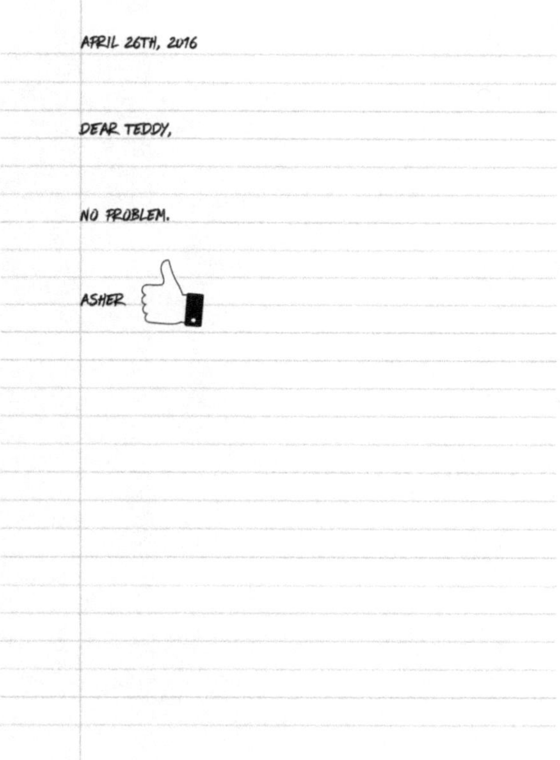

***

Thanks so much for making it all the way to the end of part one of Teddy and Asher's story! We so hope you devoured it! Before you go, we'd love if you could leave a few short words of what you thought of F*THS! Make sure you review and tell others what you thought. Again, thank you for your purchase and be sure to flip through the end pages to discover more addictive reads from G.L. Tomas. Happy Reading!

G.L. Tomas is a twin writing duo and lover of all things blerdy, fearless and fun. When they're not spending their time crafting swoon-worthy heroes, they're battling alien forces in other worlds but occasionally take days off in search mom and pop spots that make amazing pasteles and tostones fried to perfection.

They host salsa lessons and book boyfriend auditions in their secret headquarters located in Connecticut.

Head over to our Official website @ GLTomaswrites.com There we have a list of our upcoming titles and you can purchase our paperbacks directly, along with other swag!

Think this was the last you've seen of Asher and Teddy? Did Teddy really say goodbye? Stay tuned to see how their future looks in *Friends That Still...* You can also hop on over to our official *F*THS Pinterest board* to see our fantasy casts and dream-ups of the characters!

Sign up for G.L. Tomas' newsletter.

You'll get exclusives, such as book release updates, chances to win or earn free swag, access to well thought-out book lists, and opportunities to save on books before anyone else!

Don't forget to connect with us on Bookbub and our exclusive Facebook Group! And be sure to send us an email to talk books and about your fave characters! Drop us a line at guinevere.libertad@gltomaswrites.com

If you liked reading F*THS as much as we did writing it, please consider leaving a review! Reviews are a huge part of how other readers discover and judge a book. It may seem like such a small gesture but it's a small gesture that goes a long way and makes the book you loved come up in more also bought searches and has the chance to be featured in consumer newsletters.

Just a quick "I loved this book" is praise enough and encourages your favorite writers to churn out that next favorite read. So don't be shy, if you enjoyed reading, a review would mean the world for a relatively new book! Follow this link to leave a review!

AVAILABLE FOR PRE-ORDER: THE ENGAGEMENT PLAN

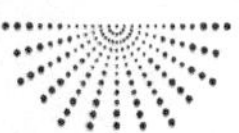

BOOK TWO OF THE LOVE UNEXPECTED SERIES

Evan Cattaneo was used to getting what he wanted.

THE SUCCESSFUL CAREER. **Check.**

. . .

THE PENTHOUSE APARTMENT overlooking the city. **Check.**

LET'S not forget the drop-dead gorgeous girlfriend. **Triple Check.**

ONLY NOW, being in the relationship of his dreams, he discovers one slight problem that puts a dent in his plans for the future. His girlfriend Luz doesn't see herself getting hitched.

FORCING Evan to confront their differences and understand their conflicting ideas.

THE ENGAGEMENT PLAN.

A TRIP ACROSS THE COUNTRY, some much-needed therapy and their ability to work together as a couple fit into that neat little package. Only the closer he comes to uncovering the truth behind her reasons, he learns a devastating secret that will affect the state of their once happy union.

Pre-order now!

AVAILABLE FOR PRE-ORDER: MELT FOR YOU

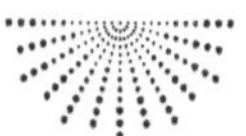

BOOK TWO OF THE KINKY MATCHMAKER SERIES

Leomie Coutard was looking to create a fresh start. New place, new job prospects, the task she's yet to conquer? Her non-existent love life. Considering her unique taste, sadly, not just any guy would do.

SHE MET the man of her dreams presenting at a kink conference a year ago, but being oceans apart forced their two-week long connection to come to an end. Or did it?

DAMIEN KARAGIANNIS COULDN'T BELIEVE his luck. Settling into a different country and a new practice left him less time to meet people, let alone date. Through a wicked twist of fate, he not only gets the chance to reconnect to his budding Dominant stranger through matchmaker Mistress Alice she ends up being a part of his surgical team.

LEOMIE CAN'T GET the intimidatingly sexy surgeon out of her system. Damien craves that soft command he once explored. Their undeniable passion will have them breaking all their rules for each other.

MELT For You is a steamy May/December romance that features a gentle Domme with an appetite for masochism and an arrogant yet romantic male submissive who wants nothing but to make her wishes come true. It is BWWM with no cheating and a guaranteed HEA. If Dominance and submission aren't your style, sit this one out. If you like a little kink, let this Alpha submissive melt his way into your heart!

<u>Pre-order now!</u>

Love Unexpected Series:
Love finds even those not looking!
The Love Bet
The Engagement Plan(Pre-order now)
The Hook-Up Games (sign up to our mailing list to learn more!)

Kinky Matchmaker Series:
Kinksters find their perfect naughty match!
Meant For You
Melt For You (Available for Pre-order)
More For You(sign up to learn when it drops)

Friends That Have Sex Series:
A love pessimist and gentle bad boy can't get enough of each other...
F*THS (Also available in audio)
Friends That Still... (Also available in audio)
Friends That Collide (sign up to learn when it drops)

. . .

Bookish Friends To Lovers Series:
Book lovers find they have more than enough in common to take it there despite the circumstances.
Same Page (Also available in audio)
Next Chapter (Coming soon to audio)
Pagebreak (sign up to learn when it drops)
Bookmark (sign up to learn when it drops)